By the same author in Mandrake

History of Fun, Book 1

Author website

www.maryhedger.com

occult high

history of fun, book 2

mary hedger

Mandrake of Oxford

Copyright © 2004
Mary Hedger and Mandrake of Oxford
First English Edition

Published by:
Mandrake of Oxford
PO Box 250
Oxford
OX1 1AP
www. mandrake.uk.net

A CIP catalogue record for this book is available from the British Library and the US Library of Congress.

ISBN 1869928733 hardback, 1869928334 paperback

Printed and bound by Lightning Source

to LSTS

∴ one

1.1 The Abbey of Love

Behind the village the mountain rose to a great height in jagged contour; although of course, what could be seen was the first slope of many that made up the mountain. There was not much life on the slopes except a few goats, olive groves and an occasional poet. The main settlement was by the sea where the people fished and grew fruit and vegetables in the alluvial soil by the river.

For all the hill's infertility the sun glowed none the less bright, the sea looked none the less gorgeous and the moon was bigger than money. The smell of oregano perfumed each footfall with subtle sensory delight, although earth here was anorexic - barely fleshed.

This was Cefalù on the north coast of the sullen land of Sicily, by the Mediterranean Sea. Here came Beast and his Company, to settle upon the hill, a four mile ascent from the village by the sea, accessible only by foot or mule.

Beast climbed up the hill, jumping from rock to rock to get a view out to sea. This was a location where his fantasies could flourish. He could be sea-cavorting Neptune or rock-bounding Pan; then at the top of the world, Jahveh, monotheistically the one and only.

'Ipsissimus,' Beast whispered to the sea. 'I am he, I have come.' It was a perfect moment.

'Ipsissimus is not enough. I must be the fountain of my own belief. Godhead.'

'I am! I am!' He stretched his arms out to his sides and then above his head. His simple grey robe fell around him in statuesque folds and blended with the rocks that poked up through the grass like bones through flesh. The sky was pure blue as he spoke to the mountain.

'I have come so far in my soul to become what I knew myself to be in my heart. I have absorbed all forbidden territories into my being. I understand all the intelligent codes etched on the gates to the labyrinth of knowledge. I have not flinched at any danger that must be overcome along the pathway of wisdom.

'I have sacrificed memory for instinct,
I have given sobriety in exchange for passion,
My courage has been rewarded
By memory and sobriety being returned
In greater measure than the measure of my sacrifice.

'I am Ipsissimus. Yet I need godhead, in order that my ego and the divine become as one and I become a man embodying the entire history of mankind. In my uniqueness, let divine power enter my body in light power and in dark power. Make me brimful of Love. In this manner shall our Abbey prosper.'

Beast raised his arms and face to the sun. His ceremonial grey bishop's hat (marked with a golden pentacle) fell off his head. A giggle came from the brow of the hill. Claudia had been watching him. Beast stood unmoved, receiving the sun's hot rays within him as pure power for his Great Work and the prosperity of his Abbey of Love.

Rather hot, Claudia scrambled to join him; she picked up his grey hat, shaped like a pirate's.

'Put this on. Otherwise you'll get sunstroke.'

Beast clapped his hands, thrice, loudly and then thanked Claudia for the proffered hat which he placed upon his head with priestly gesture, ridiculously pompous in this radiant outdoor setting.

Claudia stamped her bare feet upon the scratchy herbs and breathed in the aroma thus released.

'Est says you should wear a hat with a brim, otherwise

your nose will go bright red then peel off entirely. A wide brim like mine.' She twirled her straw hat on a finger; a flick of the wrist sent it spinning, 'Catch!' she called to Beast, who automatically reached one arm up, but the sun flashed in his eyes and he missed.

'If you had been wearing a hat with a brim,' said Claudia primly, 'you could have caught that.' She grabbed her hat. 'Race you to the top.' She tucked her white skirt into her knickers and ran.

Beast was unsure how to react, unused to following another's initiative. Claudia realised he was not following. 'Come on, race you. Or can't you climb mountains?'

'Of course I can!' he shouted and lifted up his grey robe. He dashed off, his skinny nimble legs managing the rocks very well. She waited for him and then joined him in a mad dash to the top.

'I feel as if I could dive off this mountain top and slip into sheets of sea.' Beast offered himself to nature. Breathing heavily, Claudia stretched her arms above her head, mimicking Beast's earlier posture. 'You are quite fit really, aren't you?'

'Ha ha ha ha!' Beast laughed.

They walked companionably. 'I'm thirsty. Why do they call you Beast?'

'Because I am the Beast. Don't drink the water here; it would make you sick.'

'Why are you the Beast?'

He fixed the monstrous shine of his eyes upon her.

'They call me the Beast for that was the name my mother gave me. Wherever I go, whatever I do and however I evolve, I will always be Beast.'

Claudia rubbed her eyes as if salt had been poured into them.

'I shan't call you Beast.'

'What shall you call me?'

'What's your real name?'

'My real name?' Playing for time.

'Yes, your real name,' Claudia insisted.

'My real name died a long time ago. You may call me God if you wish.'

'God?' Claudia wrinkled up her nose indignantly. 'God is not a name, God is supernatural.'

'Why not God? Can't a man also be a supernatural being?' Beast asked, treating Claudia as an equal.

'Man cannot be God because man dies and God does not.'

'Not all parts of a man die,' asserted Beast as the Abbey of Love appeared before them.

'Maybe not. But not any of God ever dies. I will not call you God. I shall call you nothing at all until you tell me your real name.'

'Nothing at all will do very well.'

Claudia, seeing Est at the well in the front yard of the .

Abbey of Love, ran off to help her wind the bucket up. This was how all the water for the Abbey of Love was provided.

The Abbey was three crude shacks around a rough mud yard in the centre of which was the well where Est and Claudia drew water. The shacks were rustic and quaint in the morning sunshine, their faults and drawbacks as residences glamorised by the optimism of this morning.

It was thrilling to live together as a family though without blood tie. There were many different relationships to explore, so many different ways to give and receive and such offspring expected.

1.2 Inside the Shacks

'I don't know what Maltby will think of this set-up.' Est rested the canvas bucket on the earth, before carrying it into the makeshift kitchen that she and Miss Jane had established.

'Why? Is he coming?' Claudia spun around at the idea, her orange skirt lifting with the movement. Her ungroomed blond locks fell in rats' tails across her face.

'No, he's not coming.' With firm hand Est pushed open a rough wooden door into a shack, little more than a cowshed. A stone floor gave way to earth in places; rough wooden rafters supported a rush roof.

'Not *ever* coming?' Claudia shoved open the next door for Est, which fell off a hinge and banged Est on the head. 'Maltby could mend the door,' Claudia suggested.

'We'll take it off, we don't need a door here.' Est set down the bucket in this room that she'd begun to turn into a kitchen and dining room. As yet there were simply two dirt engrained trestle tables facing each other.

'Are we really going to stay here forever?' asked Claudia as they scrubbed a table with large hard bristled brushes. It took a good deal of arm strength to move a scrubbing brush up and down to clean out all the ingrained dirt.

'Come on, let's carry this outside,' Est suggested, seeing how much dirt was coming off the table. They collapsed the folding legs and took the table into a piece of shade beside the shack to continue their work. They sluiced water off the table and the wood began to reveal its natural light colour.

'We aren't really going to stay here forever, are we?' asked Claudia again, hot and thirsty. 'It isn't a house!'

Est laughed, joy in the musical notes of her laughter. 'No! It is *not* a house.'

'Where are you going to paint Est? You are going to paint, aren't you?' Claudia queried.

Her mother replied, 'There are other things in the world beside painting.'

'Like what - apart from me?'

With scrubbing brush in one hand, Est observed Beast's elegant gait as he seemed to slide across the mud yard to enter the shack he was developing for ceremonial purposes. This meant he chanted to the four directions, while Pet and Miss Jane alternately squabbled and rearranged the ceremonial furniture that Mama Shag had sent.

The placement of the altar finally decided on, it was the light now which was not right. One window must be curtained, then another and then of course the holes in the ramshackle roof had to be repaired.

'Every single drop of light must be eliminated,' Beast insisted. 'I do not want my black to look purple nor for any of you to see either the colour of my eyes or the size of my pupils, unless I wish it.

'You have spent too long already upon that roof. I do not believe you are concentrating. Let me help you. Come here, Pet. You too Miss Jane, this will be new for you.' Beast grasped her firmly by the shoulders and gazed deeply into her eyes. His idea of "help" was not practical. She shuddered, sexually aroused. Beast moved his sure hands to her breasts, still fixing her with his compelling gaze. He moved his hands down her body to her stomach, one hand grasped her mount of Venus.

Wanting penetrative sex, she shut her eyes.

'Open your eyes Miss Jane.' She seemed unable to obey. 'Now.' His voice was colder than an iron dildo, as cold as thwarted passion. Miss Jane opened her eyes. Outside Est and Claudia continued scrubbing that kitchen table.

'We shall have to do something about your name. Pet!' he called, 'Hurry up, you. Bring the tooled Moroccan case. "Miss Jane" hardly suits you now and will not suit you at all within a week. There is much work we can do here that would be impossible within the bosom of civilisation.'

At the word "bosom", Miss Jane closed her eyes again.

'Open your eyes,' repeated Beast. 'First you shall be witness and then we shall decide what will happen to you. Witness Pet's punishment for tardiness at his work.'

Pet handed Beast a beautiful leather case. Beast laid it down carefully upon the rough ground. He clicked open the catches of the case and lifted the leather lid. 'Ah.' He licked his lips as if selecting a chocolate from a ribbon-wrapped selection box. Curled up neatly inside was a multi-stranded cat-o-nine-tails and the thick plait of a demon lash. Beast selected the cat; he tickled the palm of his hand with its strands and then with a flick of the wrist he skilfully wound the fine leather tails around his wrist. The smooth damp touch of leather belied the sharp, urgent sting of the whip.

Miss Jane gasped in shock, though she was easily held by Beast's charisma and there was no doubt that she would stay in the Ceremonial Shack to witness Pet's thrashing.

'A week of this and you'll not be so prim yourself,' Beast assured her.

She longed for penetrative sex, her yoni was wet and throbbing. Her face bore that particularly open and voracious expression of a woman crazy for cock.

Beast instructed her, 'You must kiss him first, fulsomely upon the lips. Kiss to exchange saliva, wind your tongue around his, explore his teeth and his gums and the soft patches of tender flesh behind wet lips. Explore Pet's mouth. Press your lips against his. Arouse him.'

*   *   *

Three shacks constituted the Abbey of Love. In the Ceremonial Shack a cat cut a thousand small cuts across

Pet's back and Miss Jane longed for penetrative sex. The second shack was known as the Kitchen Shack, where stood one clean table. Est and Claudia now carried the second table into the yard for scrubbing. Est sang heartily to hide the slaps and moans coming from the Ceremonial Shack; she did not want Claudia to hear them.

Est raised her eyes to heaven and used her strong painter's arm upon the trestle table. The sun had passed its midday peak. She was hungry but wasn't sure what food they had. Perhaps she should go down to the village and buy some bread, cheese and tomatoes?

In the third shack, straw covered the floor. Bedclothes lay tossed and tangled where the Prophets of Love had slept entwined the previous night. Est and Claudia slept somewhat apart from the others, who made strange utterances in the night, sounds which frightened Claudia.

One bundle of bedding moved and the creature within rolled on to her back. She rubbed her nose and snorted. Animal's face was bruised and swollen. Still sleeping, she scratched the flea bites on her legs. She sniffed, snorted and turned over. She burrowed in the animal feed sacks she used as bedding, trying to shade her eyes from the sun coming in from the window, a crude shuttered opening in the wall.

Animal scratched. Her dress had rucked up around her waist and her naked hip-bone touched cold stone. A straw quill scraped her tender eyelid.

She sat up and dragged a feed sack across her lap. She patted the straw, searching for her red dream diary.

'June 14th 19___' she wrote. 'It has taken us all winter to find this place and now we are here we move slowly and uncertainly. It is as if our heads were shrouded in layer upon layer of cobweb, clouding our minds.

'Beast smokes continuously and is obsessed with the Magickal Child: he hopes I shall become pregnant soon and bear the Offspring of Love. He has resumed his experiments with heroin.

'Dream: I have taken a series of shortcuts in a maze. I did this by attacking the structure of the maze itself. As a rat will chew through cardboard, so I bit into the walls either side of me, walls so high I could not see their limits. The more I looked up the higher they seemed. I felt very small. I was too lazy to travel up either one of the two corridors extending in opposite directions. I knew I could find my way out if I tried, but there seemed no point. All that lay beyond this maze was only another game I would have to play.

'The walls were bright red and sticky and when I licked them they tasted sweet. I pressed my nose up to a wall, it smelt of strawberries. I scraped the wall with my teeth and chewed off lumps, thus making a hole by which I hoped to escape the maze. It wasn't until I had sunk in up to my ankles that I realised the floor was giving way.

'I worried that I would not be able to reach the hole I had

made in the wall, I was sinking so fast. Desperately I hammered on the wall. The harder I hammered the more I sank. The wall hardly vibrated, it had to be very thick.'

'Animal!' Miss Jane called. 'Animal!

'I'm writing my diary,' Animal muttered under her breath, barely audibly. She quickly finished the diary entry:

'I bit into the floor and walls again. I lost interest in leaving the maze, even forgot I was in a maze. I felt sick from eating so much sugar. I curled up to sleep in the strawberry sweetmeat.

'In a factory somewhere, sweets were made in the shape of my curled body. I saw a girl unwrapping one of these sweets. Her head was very big, her face sticky; she smiled as she chewed.' Animal slammed the red diary shut.

'Animal!' called Miss Jane. 'Animal!'

'I'm here. I'm coming. Let me find my knickers. I can't find my knickers. I'm coming with no knickers on.'

'Animal!'

'I'm coming, just let me find my hairbrush. No, I can't find my hairbrush only straw and insects, ugh! Insect bites.' Animal sprang up out of the straw, leapt through the door and ran across the yard.

'Come on!' Animal, on fire with bites, implored Miss Jane. 'Come to the sea.' Her bare feet ran on the dry mud track. She leapt unevenly each time she stepped on a knobbly stone.

Miss Jane watched her go and glanced sideways to the

shed where she had witnessed Pet's whipping. The excitement and repulsion of it had taken her spontaneity from her. She couldn't do anything without thinking about it first. She'd noticed before that Beast and his goings-on had that effect on her.

Animal took the left fork to the beach rather than the right to the village and zigzagged out of sight.

The door to the Ceremonial Shack burst open and Pet came running out, his back on fire, blood dripping down his skinny buttocks. His thighs were so thin that Miss Jane could see his penis and heavy testicles hanging between them from behind, slapping this way and that as he followed Animal down to the beach. Miss Jane was slow and thoughtful, surprised how fast he ran, how much energy he had.

Est and Claudia's rhythmic cleansing of tables continued as Beast joined Miss Jane in the doorway. He was as lifeless and meaningful as a symbol in his grey robe, revealed as shabby and thin in the relentless sun.

'A monument, a man who has absorbed the earth perhaps?' Miss Jane wondered cocking her head on one side, in manner of a well fattened pheasant.

Beast and Miss Jane regarded one another. She waited to see if he would move first. Of course he would not. With humble hanging head and small step she moved towards him. Her hands were clasped together in front of her. Beast stepped aside to let her pass into the Ceremonial Shack and then followed her in, shutting out the sound of the table being scrubbed behind them, shutting out that reminder of domestic regularity.

It was cool and dark in the Ceremonial Shack for the shutters had been closed all day. Fuzzy bands of light seeped in around the edges of doors and windows. The smell of fresh animal lingered in the air. If she could have seen that far, Miss Jane would have noticed a phial of fresh blood standing upon the now erected altar, inbetween the bell and the sword and in front of the great jewelled goblet. The book of grimoires was stored high up upon a shelf above the altar out of casual reach.

Beast would penetrate her now, she hoped.

1.3 Words of Truth

For the time being, Beast's focus was Animal. He paid little attention to Miss Jane, who had to content herself with some idle masturbation. Animal soon returned from bathing with Pet; Beast was ready for her. He wanted to record his ideas and magickal reckonings before engaging in the sexmagickal act that would beget a Magickal Child.

'The time of inspiration is past. The time of sacred action has come. We must sleep little and practice our magick with enthusiasm on this hot hill,' Beast intoned.

Animal was alive only for his Will to flood her consciousness, as he had trained her to be.

'This is a time from which the world shall never look back. Our way of magick supersedes all systems that have gone before. All philosophies and beliefs merge and become one through the scope of my being.

'Come Animal, I shall dictate.'

He arranged himself cross legged upon a dirty black

velvet cushion and puffed on his curvaceous pipe. Animal sat by the pile of paper (work in progress), and lit a small candle which she set in a tall candlestick, to make light to write by.

'There shall be no dancing until I have found the magickal rhythm for a new dance, unique to our Abbey of Love. Likewise there shall be no music until the music of the spheres descends into my very being.

'A night shall come, when alien moon energy will accumulate in your body. And on that night we all shall penetrate you, Animal. We shall fill your body with the elixir of Love in a celebration of Love. A Magickal Child shall come to your womb; its parents shall be Place and Time and its spirit shall be the Will of God. I shall be God.'

He paused to smoke and allow Animal time to write his words in full.

'We ought to put a date. Do you know the date?' He asked her. Animal shrugged.

'You do know the date,' Beast insisted. 'You have been writing daily in your magickal diary.'

She flashed her eyes angrily at him, convinced that he had been reading her diary.

'If you cannot remember the date, you must get your red diary and find it. But I think you do remember it. You do, do you not Animal?'

She nodded, a minimalist gesture.

'I have lived my life backwards.' Beast continued

complacently. 'I was born an old man and grew to the innocence of a newborn babe. My life encompasses the cultural and religious history of mankind. I inherited complete knowledge and I have worked my way through it, testing it with ritual magick. Now that process is complete and I am a Babe of the Abyss, I am ready to begin the new history of man. This is a time that can be conceptualised only in the present moment, which is why I describe a moment as a *history*, encompassing all.'

In spite of the gloom in the shack, Beast's pupils were pinpricks from heroin usage.

'Life moves around ordinary mortals, not so myself: life moves within me, for I am life. I have climbed the mountains of this earth, have swam its seas, have learnt the secrets that this planet holds. I have lived through the cataclysmic fears that knowledge brings. I have survived exploration of the physical and the occult realms of this life and have transcended mortal expectation.

'By the way, Animal, what do you think of Miss Jane? Are you jealous?'

Animal shrugged, pen poised to continue writing. The solitary candle spat and spluttered.

'The candle is more honest than you,' Beast laughed seductively, his voice mesmeric as his syllables ran into one another. 'She shall be named and be fully one of us. Then you shall truly know her and the energy of your jealousy will transform to pure Love.'

'Shall I write that down?' Animal hardly concealed her bitterness. Beast's laughter was soothing and exciting. Like passionate love, it drew her to him whatever her mood.

'I am opposed to tradition, yet encompass all rituals of all peoples. I have achieved this through study and experience; but the work I have done upon my very being is of ultimate importance. I have erased all social conditioning. My soul is free to travel in the ether. My body is free to express its passions liberated from emotion yet encompassing all possible emotions, both extreme and subtle. I am the result of a potent alchemy of being and this alchemy I have accomplished through magick.

'I am perennially ancient and perennially newborn: I am a Babe of the Abyss.' He paused to draw on his smouldering pipe.

'Excuse me.' Animal rushed out of the door, holding her stomach. As sunlight hit her retina, she threw up. Acidic orange bile burnt her mouth. She staggered towards the well to rinse out her mouth, accidentally putting a bare foot in her own slimy vomit.

At the well she fumbled with the winch, but could not operate the bucket. She let go of the handle and suddenly released, the bucket clattered down the shaft banging against the sides, before it hit the water at the bottom, luckily still attached to its rope.

Est looked up from the newly cleaned table. Animal was a mystery to her, she had never seen her do anything ordinary; nor did she chat or gossip.

Animal retched again, though spat out but a small globule of acidic gastric juice.

'Go and buy some cheese from the goatherd darling,' Est asked Claudia, putting some coins in her daughter's hand. Est drew a bucketful of water for Animal who leant against the brickwork of the well, unable to properly function. Est handed her a cup of water. Animal rinsed her mouth and spat. She swallowed a little water, but this only made her heave again.

'You're not alright are you?' Est suggested.

Animal ignored her and staggered back into the Ceremonial Shack. Est collapsed the trestle table and hauled it into the makeshift kitchen, wondering if there was anything there that might soothe Animal's stomach. 'She is a woman who has lost most of herself and doesn't realise she'll never find a substitute for that self,' Est thought, while also thinking about pictures to paint. But she could not imagine picking up a paintbrush with so many jobs to do to maintain routine hygiene and nutrition.

'The work is hard and we shall continue deep into the night,' Beast informed as Animal returned to paper and pen.

'You must always bear in mind and feel within your heart, that the definition of your soul lies easily within the extent of my being. Any rebellion will upset you, may even make you ill.' And in a gentler tone, 'My devoted Animal, put on your brown woollen gown and let us dedicate this altar.

'We shall use a system of colours as our symbolic tool. Each colour shall represent an emotion. Pastel shades represent diluted and tranquil emotion, darker hues signify the disturbing intensity of raw reaction.

'Red is anger, ranging from inspiration that leads to action to explosive destructive power.

'Green is jealousy, also growth. Yellow, cowardice in its weaker form, when rich and golden it is bravery.

'Blue is always harmonious, but excess can indicate stagnation. Brown is satisfied need when red brown, greed when dark and when beige, variously refinement or inhibition.

'Purple is demure when mauve, coy in lilac and regally self-assured in the fullness of its darkest hue.'

Beast turned the ring of Nuit upon the sun finger of his right hand. He twisted his forelock to stand up horn-like upon his forehead.

'We shall dedicate this altar. Put on your brown woollen cloak and reveal the mark of the Beast between your breasts. Ring the bell for astral silence and ring it again to invite the wealth of astral colour into our Abbey. When that is done I shall invoke the angels of Love and the demons of my heart to reveal themselves. When all is done, we shall see what we shall see.'

1.4 Miss Jane's Degradation

The Abbey of Love espoused an untaught reality, a reality received via visions and as such not open to discussion or revision. It was established as a mirror image of the universe.

Beast's visions, these days, were induced by cocaine, heroin and hashish and facilitated by alcohol, a poisonous combination. Beast believed physical poison did not affect spiritual clarity, for didn't the great seers instruct that the body's desires must be transcended?

He used drugs as an immediate road to knowledge, considered them the fast track to the deep waters of the subconscious and as such the staple food of magick. He had trained himself specifically not to think in terms of cause and effect. He trusted the sensual enthusiasm he cultivated within himself.

Times between the highs were flat times of sickness and despondency that he accepted in anticipation that the next high would probe more profoundly into the mysteries of true Will.

Beast had dropped off in the middle of dictating to Animal. Such *gouching out* is common among heroin users. Listless, Animal was no less willing to dip her fingers in the heroin and cocaine pie. Mama Shag's was a place of purity compared to the squalor at the Abbey of Love.

Est kept her distance from Beast. Especially she kept Claudia out of his way, often sending her on errands to the village. Here Claudia played with the village children and learnt some Italian.

Est watched Beast; observed how little he moved and how little he did. She watched the comings and goings from the Ceremonial Shack where he held court. Very occasionally in daylight he staggered out to urinate, usually at great length and with obvious satisfaction. Twice, she had watched him raise his grey robe and squat, with his back supported by the shack's wall, to defecate. He'd wiped his anus on his robe before retreating back into the gloom of the Ceremonial Shack.

Miss Jane lived in a state of anxious expectation. She had given over her entire fortune to Beast to found this Abbey of Love and felt she had, as yet, very little to show for her investment. 'Except for the shagging,' she would say to herself when calculating her losses and gains through her commitment to Beast.

Miss Jane and Beast had met in Paris. He had immediately impressed her with his regal bearing and charisma and she'd fallen for him. After a few drinks (that she'd paid for) she followed him to a luxurious hotel where they'd stayed in sexual embrace for ten days and ten nights. Though day or night she'd hardly known nor cared; the curtains had remained closed the entire time.

They had eaten little, drunk much. From time to time a messenger arrived with curious small packages Beast would accept with great relish.

Like an automaton, she'd found herself paying for this ten day hotel sojourn too, she hadn't dared suggest he should contribute. He, with his jewels and silk robes, expensive habits and rich mistresses, he who had been further East than her dreams and guzzled the rarest fine wines in the world, he seemed rich. She didn't know that actually he had exhausted his inheritance.

For ten days he'd ravished her. She had knelt on all fours and shown him her vulva and anus, offered them to him for the pleasure of his fabulous lingam. She had done whatever he proposed. He'd shagged her anus and her mouth. Lord! Shagged her anus before even touching her yoni. She couldn't even think about it. Especially now she had so much time to think about it, for he hadn't touched her for days. He hadn't parted her legs nor plunged into her with his rod of power and she missed it badly.

Miss Jane sobbed quietly behind the communal sleeping quarters. No one heard her and no one comforted her.

1.5 A Demon Comes

Beast's voice filled the rustic shack as Animal continued
to take dictation.

'In the shadow of the Great Pyramid the Book of Law
was received. Demon after demon materialised to give up
its offering to the Great Book while Irene, the seer,
announced each one's name and purpose. With each
demon my penis became stiffer until verily, I believed the
stories I had heard about a yogi suspending eight bricks
from his lingam. Irene was transfixed by my lingam. First as
it stirred my robe and then when I tore the robe from my
hot demon crazed body. She licked her burning lips and her
breasts heaved.

'We had been married for six months and six months of
debauch had prepared her well for her job as seer. I had not
expected such superb results, had not hoped for anything
like that when I'd married her. In fact it was more or less an
accident that I had.

'Don't write that down.' Beast leant to one side, and stuffed his pipe with fresh tobacco.

'Mundane facts are out of place in a magickal summary, the mind of the reader must be kept concentrated upon the plane of the paranormal. By consistency and repetition the paranormal will gradually unfold within the reader's mind, introducing him to Shadowland. Here, demons cavort with satyrs and the notes upon the pipes of Pan are as the letters of a demonic alphabet spelling out the wisdom of unbound life!'

Beast smoked contentedly. He scratched an itch in the small of his back.

'Plump up my cushions, rub my back, send for Pet,' he whined. 'Bring me some black eyeliner and perfume. Where is Pet?'

Animal stroked her vulva absentmindedly. 'I don't think he'll come,' she spoke to the rafters. 'I can't see him sodomising you either, if that's what you're after.'

Beast couldn't be bothered to be angry. 'Animal, have you been masturbating as much as you can? Come here.'

Animal sat lightly on Beast's chest, lifted her skirt and pulled apart her labia to show him her clitoris.

'Nearer,' he commanded. She swung her strong sex-seer's thighs and sat on Beast's face. Beast tongued her clitoris, her sex juice left a lascivious trail over his smirking visage.

As they were thus engaged, a silent figure entered the

room and stood quietly to one side, curious about what went on in here. It was gloomy in the Ceremonial Shack, but it just looked like more S-E-X. Beast's tongue probed Animal's vagina, then her anus, then along the tiny length of her erect clitoris. He squeezed and slapped her buttocks.

'We are ready,' Beast intoned, 'to ask my demons to manifest their glamour within our Abbey. Pour wine, mix it with blood and we will drink.'

The quiet figure, with her back against the wall, watched as Beast ran his hands up and down Animal's body as she mixed the two red liquids, wine and blood that sprang freshly from knife cuts she'd made on her thumbs.

He pressed the contours of her body, stroked her almost bare bones with the fat palms of his hands. Her spine was loose and excited, mobile under Beast's Will.

'Love and Immortality,' toasted Beast and drank from a jewelled pewter goblet he then handed to Animal. They drank the large pitcher dry, drank until they swooned. They lay in an ecstatic entangled heap until a rosy light seeped into the room. As far as the watching Claudia could tell, the light emanated from a black hole in the air. The light had a sense of purpose and destination, was seemingly from another dimension. It seeped in to the ritually prepared space dot by red dot, whirled around at great speed and exploded into a mass of brilliant orange flames. The light itself was a burning entity, with a fiery and frightening brilliance. Claudia was worried that it would touch her and harm her.

Suddenly, the black hole closed as if an aperture of a camera snapped shut. Several flickering tongues of flame remained and hung, crackling, in the air before the altar, above the entangled Beast and Animal. Claudia shook with terror. As they burnt, the flames twisted into the shape of a demon with two empty black holes for eyes. As she watched, a huge phallus formed from bright gold fire and spat out showers of sparks over the two figures. The demon crackled with life, a dense fireball of energy. It didn't speak, but Claudia knew it was communicating something, for there was rhythm in its roaring flames and golden sparks.

The golden sparks accumulated around Animal's navel and she twisted to throw them from her.

Animal prodded Beast in the ribs. 'Wake up. The first demon is here. Wake up,' she repeated. 'Demon Fire has come.' Animal's voice dropped one and a half octaves, to become the demon's voice; she was possessed.

'Wake Beast. I am Jupiter, demon-god residing in your scrotum. I am divine lightning.'

Beast rolled over and snored loudly. His bare bottom was saggy and pathetic; rhinoceros folds of flesh hung under the buttocks.

'I knew you'd come,' Beast mumbled and then suddenly sat up, electrified. His eyes as fiery as the demon's, his mouth opened, 'What?'

'It is the demon,' Animal's voice was deep and alien. 'The demon is with you.'

The light that had come from the black hole was living fire; it danced around Beast's head penetrating his mind. Beast clutched his temples; his features contorted with agony.

'It hurts,' Beast moaned.

'It is supposed to hurt.' Animal in the deep sub-human demon voice.

Beast's tongue hung out of his mouth. His penis was so hard, it throbbed painfully. A green light, like liquid radioactivity, began to flow from the two black holes of the demon's eyes. The holes were footprint-shaped.

'You have seen red and you have seen orange. Now we are green and if you do not readily take us into your mind, your life will be invalid. Absorb us and you will be inexpressibly empowered.

'Absorb the green footprints,' Animal possessed by demonic fire ordered.

'It hurts,' moaned Beast wanting to hear, "it's supposed to hurt" again, which really turned him on.

'Move away from pain. Lay claim to ten demons.' Animal's demonic voice invaded Beast's kidneys and heart and moved him away from pain.

Beast was aware of his soul, white and radiant, moving out of his body. The two green footprints in front of the altar marked the entrance to another dimension. Beast's ethereal body folded into a ball of light which accelerated rapidly towards the green footprints, passing through them. In turn they folded in upon themselves and vanished into the black hole, deleting Beast's soul.

Claudia ran from the room, leaving the door ajar behind her. Animal slumped next to Beast's lifeless body. Both Animal and Beast were inert lumps, as sacks of potatoes are.

∴ two

2.1 Things to Do in the Morning

In the small hours Beast drifted off into a heroin stupor, when a slow heartbeat lulled his body into a state of dreaming awake.

'Ah!' Beast clutched his throat. 'It is red, it is all red.' He clawed at his cheeks and eyes, trying to pull suffocating red mucus off his face. He imagined his flabby cheeks were bright red with his long tongue hanging out, blue about the edges. 'It is all red, I cannot breathe.' The back of his throat gurgled as he felt warm menstrual blood bubbling in his mouth, scorching his lungs as he gasped for air.

Beast's throat was paralysed, he could not make another sound; he felt mucus solidifying inside his lungs, steadily cementing up his bronchioles.

Animal shivered in the infested straw.

'Am I dead or alive?' thought Beast, and of course there was only one possible answer to this question, for where there's thought there's life. Yes! He was alive! Plus many more exclamation marks.

Beast was perennially either under the positive influence of heroin, that is beatific tranquillity, or under its negative influence - under pressure and climbing up the wall in heroin withdrawal. Unable to sit still, itching under his scalp and beneath his belly button, itching in impossible places that couldn't be touched yet screamed, "touch me touch me." Aching joints cried out in agony for heroin ASAP.

'Animal, get me some more heroin.'

'What?' she answered sleepily.

'I need my grey and brown powdered bliss.' Even in pain Beast had time for poetry.

'I'll get Pet.'

'No, not Pet. You get it.'

Animal groaned and naked, wandered out of the Ceremonial Shack, into the Sleep Shack where the others slept. Est and Claudia lay to one side, Pet and Miss Jane top to tail for some reason or other. Miss Jane's toes were up Pet's arse; except she was not called that anymore, 'What did they call her?' thought Animal as she picked her way between bodies. 'After the fifth demon had come in the night that went on forever - when Est wouldn't join in - she surely had been named.'

'What had they called her? Toad? No.' Animal laughed even as she cuddled up to Pet, to sleep again. 'Not Toad. Camel? Gorilla? Oran-utan? Vomit? That could be it, Vomit.'

'More heroin Animal,' Beast called pitifully from inside the Ceremonial Shack.

As Animal buried her nose in the crevice of Pet's fleshless shoulder blade, Est stirred with the bright light of day.

'Wake up darling, let's go to town.' She wanted to check the post and buy some decent food.

'To the big town?' Claudia asked sleepily.

'Yes.'

'Hurrah!' Claudia jumped up.

'Brush your hair and wash at the well.' Est handed her a dirty battered hairbrush. Claudia made a face. 'The water's freezing.'

'It's refreshing. I'm not going to town with you covered in filth.'

'Have you got some money?' Claudia brushed her golden hair and shimmering strands moulted into the straw. Bright sunlight pierced through gaps between the rough wooden planks that formed their walls.

'I've got enough money for the bus fare.' Est scrutinised

her shoes, spat on the hem of her skirt and rubbed them with it.

'What will we buy things with?' Claudia tossed her flaxen locks from side to side.

'I'll get some from Animal.'

'*She* won't have any.'

'Really? I expect there's some at the Post Office from Maltby,' Est said confidently.

'I miss him, Mummy. When can we see Maltby? Do you mean money for your paintings? Why don't you do some paintings here?' Claudia rushed outside to dance around the well in the sunshine, too eager for life to wait for answers.

'Maybe I will buy some paints and soap, oil and flour; as much as I can carry.' Est hunted for her travelling bag to carry home shopping; shopping she hoped there would be money for.

Her men's clothes - pleated trousers, jacket and waistcoat in mid-brown wool - were folded neatly in the bottom of her travel bag, with a couple of changes of underwear. She took the garments out one by one and held them up to her nose; they smelt stale. She saw a beetle scamper in the bottom of the bag and then she saw another. She tipped the bag upside down and a hoard of hard-backed black beetles tumbled out. Their number seemed to multiply as she shook the bag. Her face flushed until the fat in her cheeks felt hot enough to melt.

She smoothed her hair, put the bag down by the well

where she drew water for herself and Claudia to wash. She wanted to look at herself in the mirror before she went into the outside world. The only mirror was in the Ceremonial Shack where Beast was blissing out. She hadn't been inside *there* since she'd got to Cefalù.

'Where are you going?' Claudia was washing her face with water.

'To look in the mirror.'

'That's a magic mirror,' Claudia assured her mother.

Apprehensively, Claudia watched her mother enter the Great Beast's lair.

'Get some heroin,' bleated out Animal from the straw, half asleep.

'Heroin,' echoed Great Beast, from the opposite shack, semi-conscious on stained velvet cushions.

Est hummed nonchalantly as she peered into the Ceremonial Shack.

'Beast? Are you there?' No reply. She looked around in the fetid gloom and found the mirror propped upon a shelf by a window. She looked at herself first from the front and then from the side. She smoothed the yellow frock printed with white flowers; she'd found it scrunched up under Animal's head as a pillow. On Abbey of Love rations, she'd become nearly as slim as Animal. She twisted the strands of her untidy fringe into small curls across her forehead, shaping them with her saliva.

'I cannot live *positively*,' Est philosophised. The corner

of the altar was reflected in the mirror next to her face. 'Positivity explores and discovers nothing; it is within negative energy where the riches of humanity are hidden. The abyss holds strange magickal memories, weird treacheries of the body and of the mind.' Est patted her coiffure, checked she had removed all dirt stains from her face and stroked her eyebrows into a vampish arch. She encouraged straggling brow hairs back into the pack.

Beast's attractive drawl came languorously from behind her:

'I steer the golden ship which crosses the ocean of discontent. Come in my ship and discover land on the other side.'

'Hum,' Est expressed doubt but was drawn to him nevertheless. Claudia had followed her and peered round the door jamb; she caught Est's eye.

'Must go,' Est to Beast briskly. 'I'll get you heroin if I can.'

Low cackle from Beast. 'You will have no problem. You are one of my creatures. The creatures of the Beast are natural players in the black market.'

'Bye for now.'

'Fare thee well, fair damsel of the day. Find my elixir, nymph of the world.'

2.2 Beast Is Deep

'Am I Great Beast?' After Beast's brief effort to entice Est he resumed his position in the straw where he regularly held court. He called his acolytes to ceremony day after day and, more importantly, for the nights that followed the days. Swooning nights when dreams themselves became afraid to reveal their tantalising symbols.

'Animal!' he roared. 'Animal!' Then, getting no response, 'Pet, was it your hooves that clasped my sides? Your rough whiskers that scratched my soft shoulder? Was it you who mounted me? Was it the elixir from your lingam that Animal sucked from my anus? Your sharp teeth that bit my neck? Your scraggy nails that etched sigils into the white canvas of my back?'

Great Beast dizzily got up on to his feet, shoved on a pair of Roman sandals. He dripped sweet rose oil on to his hands and perfumed his neck and his breast; he toyed with his nipples.

'I shall dress in splendid robes and thus magnificent shall I stir this Abbey of Love into full creative expression. This pigsty shall be transformed to a great and holy temple and our Abbey of Thelema shall thrive and prosper. Its influence shall reverberate throughout the globe. Through forest and desert, fertile plains and mysterious seas, the word of this aeon and its Thelemic manifestation shall be felt wherever there is life.

'We shall first transform this Abbey. Then we shall call followers to join us here for ceremony, secret rites and writing. First I must wake my sleeping adepts. Vomit!' He laughed to himself at the nasty name. 'Vomit! And she swallowed it! Didn't bat an eyelid when in the middle of the most solemn and sacred ceremony after thorough preparation.' He meant the sex rite. 'Didn't bat an eyelid when I said, "I name you Vomit and as Vomit shall you now spread the word of our true and holy Law, the word of Thelema." '

Beast's gorgeous saffron silk robe trailed on the ground as he moved through the courtyard. The robe was hand painted with an ingenious design of intelligent squiggles, among the initiate known as sigils.

'We shall see what we shall see,' he pondered.

He wore a shining crown, incongruous in this rustic setting. In one hand he held his ebony wand, topped with a finely cut golden topaz and in the other a richly bound volume entitled *The Book of the Law.*

He called Pet, Animal and Vomit to him and began to intone, at length, in Latin. He directed them to be insatiable. He invited them to feast with him, to annihilate the senses in sensual overload, a favourite Thelemic pastime.

'Come banquet with me,
Come enjoy exotic fruits,
Stimulating spice!

'Let us gorge on meat
Killed with our own hands,
Let us pluck chestnuts from the trees!

'Come drink
Sweet purple wine,
Feast with me on ambrosia and nectar!'

Beast rang his bell (crafted from seven metals in magickal combination). Pet and Animal did not react to this summons to ceremony but lay inert, knackered. However, hearing the donkey man, they jumped up and hugged each other. 'The hamper,' they held hands. 'The hamper!' Jubiliantly.

'Beast's been going on and on about something for hours,' Pet chatted as he stepped into a pair of loose calico pyjama bottoms.

'In Latin! Do you know what any of it means?' Animal sounded normal and well balanced, now she'd cheered up at the prospect of gourmet food, a present from one of Beast's admirers.

'A little.'

Animal looked askance.

'I did study it, when I studied Law,' Pet admitted with pride.

'You must be a genius.' Animal rummaged around but couldn't find anything to wear except a torn translucent chemise that didn't even reach her knees.

'That's where I met Beast, or Drummond as we called him then. At Cambridge,' he added after a pause.

'Have you seen my yellow dress anywhere? The one with the edelweiss? I'm sure I was using it as a pillow.' The one Est had borrowed to wear to town.

'You are a drug fuddled nymph who remembers nothing.' Pet ran his fingers through his hair, not so much to give himself a hairdo as to hunt for lice. 'Gotcha!'

'There're four hampers!' Animal declared delightedly. 'I don't care. That donkey man can think what he likes.' She strolled nonchalantly out of the shack clad in nothing but her thin translucent chemise.

She bent over to unstrap the nearest hamper and the chemise rose up her thighs. The donkey man spluttered in embarrassment torn between ogling her behind and concluding the business of unloading the hamper.

'I always have some medicine for the Doctor.' He

gestured to Beast still intoning in Latin in his sumptuous get up.

'Doctor? What Doctor? Man, look at this. There are five bottles of vintage champagne,' Pet continued. 'The old lady has done us proud.'

Animal took the brown paper package containing the "medicine" and found a few thousand lire to give the man in payment, who from experience she knew would not leave without it, as Beast never fulfilled his debts. Such was the way of the Beast and of all those who numbered themselves amongst his creatures.

2.3 Feasting Beast is Jupiter

Animal knelt in the dust with her hair falling over her face as she rummaged through the hampers. There was honey roasted cashew nuts, white Stilton, crystallised ginger, chocolate liqueurs, peppermint creams. She was dizzy with delight at sugared almonds, Carr's water biscuits, Scottish smoked salmon, young asparagus tips, plums preserved in kirsch.

Great Beast was a vision of Jupiter clad in gold as he offered his body in crucifix form to the sun - the magickal current opened. The medicine and banquet arriving together was a good sign he interpreted as meaning that more than one source of prosperity was to come.

Great Beast did not measure time in the ordinary way, so it was not possible to determine if more than one source of prosperity would reveal itself during the next, say, three weeks or even during that lunar cycle, or until midsummer. He had long since discarded the work, rest, play system of living. He'd never had a settled life. He'd broken out of the disciplined run of society as early as age twelve and had never looked back.

It was his nature was to be impassioned by one thousand simultaneous lusts and to listen to the fine details of his desire. Through magickal insight he had discovered that the power of his lust signified that he was a vehicle for divine transmission. He received higher intelligence through Aiwaz, his holy guardian angel.

Great Beast accepted the package of medicine from Animal's hand and their eyes met conspiratorially. Great Beast's confidence surged and his veins warmed; he could almost taste the goddess' elixir in his mouth, sucked from her yoni. He smacked his lips; his taste buds tingled in maximum receptivity. Hot fire churned exultantly within his belly. He bowed to Jupiter, the sun, and finished his song of invocation.

'I surrender to you Sun!
Jupiter! Fill me up with your power!

'To you Sun, I surrender,
I bask in your arms.
Fill me with Solar Power
So I, your earthly representative,
May communicate your knowledge
To human creatures.

'Hail! Jupiter! Hail! Sun!
All hail!'

Excitement loosened his bowels and the elegant Great Beast hastily found a spot to lift his robe. He wore no underclothes; he liked his holy phallus and holy balls to hang loose and free. With a groan of release he accomplished a satisfyingly complete evacuation. He rocked forward and up on to his feet without wiping his arse. 'I must bathe,' he announced to the scruffy thorn tree behind the Ceremonial Shack.

He laid the flat package of medicine upon the altar. He felt so much better now his source of heroin had been renewed. Without it, it was as though his life sap poured out of him in payment of the great debt the poppy demanded. The price of its use was absolute devotion, torn piece by piece from the fabric of one's being.

He stroked the brown paper of the package, in two minds whether to look at it now. It was not in his code of conduct to resist temptation. He opened the package. A thousand nymphs of the air flew out and softly kissed his face. He felt subliminally attractive. There was a good quantity of grey brown powder. He wetted a finger and took a dab, it was good. It was ambrosia from Jupiter to his emissary the Great Beast. Gladness filled his heart.

In came Pet; he too was partial to a walk with Jupiter.

'You have got the medicine?'

Beast ignored Pet's question. 'Pet, did I sodomise you? Or did you sodomise me?'

'When, last night? Last ceremonial?'

'No,' Great Beast was impatient. 'In the desert, in the desert when Choronzon came and scared you out of and into your wits? Did you mount me?' Pet cocked his head; he had no answer for his Master. 'Come, Pet. Accept this sacrament.'

Pet took a dab of the proffered heroin.

'Isn't it a bit early for this?' Pet was hesitant.

'It takes me time to reach ecstasy. Come, Pet. Did you spurt your seminal fluid into my anus?'

'Um, no.' Pet shuffled his feet.

'It was I who performed while you knelt, receptively?' Beast asked. 'I can't picture it.'

Pet raised an eyebrow and elaborated, 'I can envisage the joy of kneeling before the altar, my senses freed, nectar sustaining me, my white behind waiting for phallic penetration.'

'Tonight,' Great Beast was exultant, 'we will begin a new Working. I am inspired; the banquet has come. Money and devotees will follow.'

'Devotees with money,' Pet suggested.

'Vomit has spewed out her fortune and it is inadequate, like her parched crack. Have you noticed how she moons around, snivelling, without the inspiration of my phallus erect? She eats cake and cries into cream,' Great Beast said bitchily.

'My Magickal Children will come, through Vomit, Animal and the woman of small purpose, the woman, Est,'

Beast declared decisively. 'Vomit repulses me. She has a blubbering nursemaid's manner, but I will not let her oppress the spirits of our Magickal Children - begotten by Great Beast through the procreative energy of a higher intelligence.

'And you, Pet, you are as my child and I, as your father, shall willingly sacrifice my masculinity in order that you may conquer your father and become the crowned and conquering child.'

Pet raised a quizzical eyebrow.

'Didn't I tell you about the Paris Workings? Were you there?' Of course Pet had been living at No.32, in a crate in the kitchen, but did not remind Beast.

'You are the prototype Magickal Child, the blueprint of my future progeny.' Great Beast folded the packet of heroin in a silken scarf and tucked it away in one of the hidden pockets in his robe. He wandered off to where the straw was piled high behind the altar, to bliss out, peacefully drugged.

'Sleep until time comes for a satyr's horny hooves to pound upon my back and his sharp teeth to nip my flesh, all around my neck and shoulders. That woman, the woman of small purpose, she shall bring more heroin and so will begin a time of plenty. Three followers will come from the West loaded with gold.' Great Beast pulled his golden robe closely about his hips. 'Three followers shall come from the West loaded with gold,' he repeated to soothe himself. 'And we shall tear down these decrepit shacks and build a white building worthy of our Holy Order of Thelema.'

Seeing that Great Beast had zoned out into an alternate reality, Pet took the opportunity to slope off to their beach, with Animal.

Great Beast visualised the Abbey. It grew and declined within his mind. First gold tipped pink domes rose up and crumbled to reveal the clean lines of arched doorways and pillars. The pillars crumbled and the walls of the Abbey became smooth and square. In its turn the square Abbey crumbled and a nest of babies squirmed on its foundations, screaming demands at him, demands he had no intention of fulfilling. Out of his breast women were born, their breasts heavy with rich milk. Fussily they hurried to the nest of babies and quickly pacified them with swollen nipples which dripped sweet milk into their tiny mouths.

Gradually the images in Great Beast's mind relaxed into a tidal swelling and diminishment following the rise and fall of his breath. This rhythm became the momentum of a great disc spinning in the universe. Strange lights moved intelligently within the circular grooves that scoured its surface, as music is pressed into an old-fashioned LP record. Beast became a light upon the disc's surface and his body relaxed into deep sleep. He spun companionably within this UFO, while periodically an invisible waiter offered him refreshment from a mystical cup, filled with the effervescent elixir of immortality.

2.4 Vomit's Agony

Vomit laid the gourmet food out on the trestle tables. For the past fortnight she'd only eaten the mush Est swore was nourishing - if nourishing was to have a stomach achingly empty and a mouth full of ulcers! Before so much food, she was as a child waiting for permission to open her Christmas presents.

Vomit's vagina throbbed as Great Beast's phallus appeared in her mind, fulsome erect and slippery with her own sex juice. She sobbed as she remembered the other orifice that phallus had penetrated - her anus! Why ever had she let it happen? Whyever had she come here? She had given her entire life savings over to Great Beast and he had spent them on three shacks and God knew what drugs and filthy whores, infested her too into the bargain, no doubt! What a bargain! She had believed such disasters happened to other people! Now to be renamed Vomit, it was beyond the last straw.

Her dress hung off her. Her stomach and thighs used to be plump but her skin now hung empty. She didn't recognise herself. She felt she'd been branded sodomite and whore for all the world to see. How could she ever return to civilised society, and teach innocent girls as she once had done? She could barely hold her own in three humble shacks in the middle of nowhere with demons for companions. Even Est, who seemed in some ways responsible, had an unnerving look in her eye. She avoided Claudia at any cost, how could she face a former pupil?

Vomit ambled to the well. She'd eventually worked out how the bucket worked. She wound up a bucket of water and washed by the well, in public. She knew inside herself that without the props of civilisation her habits and behaviour had fallen apart. One snip and the whole knitted garment that had been Miss Jane had come undone and she was an unformed amoeba.

This was Great Beast's method, to take an acolyte away from a socially conditioned environment and throw them on to their instinct. Instinct, he reckoned, would respond and grow strong.

However, currently Vomit was a barely functioning entity whose instinct to survive had not graduated beyond the need to frequently defecate and the feeling of loss at the withdrawal of Great Beast's sexual attentions. Or rather, as he would describe it, their ritual congress. She felt personally unattractive and cast aside while he had comfortably slipped into another dimension. His finely tuned instinct preserved him from the boredom of excessive repetition; it only proved inadequate against the storm of heroin addiction, withdrawal seizures for a while in abeyance with a plentiful supply.

Beast patted his pocket and called out half in and half out of sleep, 'Vomit! We will resume congress. Prepare for the ceremonials.'

In walked Vomit right on cue, a shadow of her former self. Great Beast took her withered cheeks and kissed her full on the lips, his tongue twisting into her mouth. Her squawk was muffled as Great Beast's tongue explored her gums.

'We will open the temple and tomorrow you will write to Paris and order the sale of your school. Our Order needs you,' Beast instructed.

She hardly cared if she owned the school or not now, so unfit did she feel herself to teach.

He grasped her yoni, his middle finger finding the tight entrance to her vagina and feeling within. He removed it, it was covered in menstrual blood. His eyes brightened, 'The time is right for feasting,' he said.

She understood that he meant to perform cunnilingus on her while she menstruated. She gasped, though he knew (instinctively, intuitively, inevitably) and she knew that the temple would be opened, he would suck her blood. She would sell her school and strange visions would pass through a mind that was not her mind, yet could use her mouth to speak its Will.

And these spiritual utterances and perverted sexual practices, vile yet sacred, would elevate her soul, somehow. Through absolute degradation she would find liberation. She would do anything for so marvellous lover as Great Beast.

∴ three

3.1 A Reunion

Sicily in July; the warm evenings were lovely times of prolonged languor. Sexual murmuring came from the Ceremonial Shack. Great Beast noticed that Vomit's pubis was not so fat and juicy as when she'd been Miss Jane. He also noticed that her sexual stamina was much improved. This he considered a good omen.

He sucked upon her labia and her clitoris, paying special attention to the sensitive area either side of her love bud. He tongued her gently until every part of her genitalia was red and swollen and she was half begging him to stop. This gave him good excuse to slap her about a bit, which they both loved and made her rosy all over.

The sky was starry indeed before Pet and Animal returned from the bathing beach, fast followed by Est and Claudia returning up the track from Palermo, with none other than their good friend Maltby in tow.

Maltby hadn't heard from Est in four weeks and, rather worried, had decided to visit. He'd also take the opportunity to bring her some painting equipment and take away any new paintings to sell in Paris. He'd soon find out that she hadn't done any paintings; her time had been spent mainly in the ponderous task of caring for Claudia in primitive conditions. It was hard even to heat water on an old stove that did not draw properly, with no easy supply of fuel.

By lucky coincidence, they'd met Maltby in Palermo, which for Sicily was the big city, in a café on the seedy side of town where Est had tracked down heroin and Maltby drank and ogled sailors in closely cut trousers.

Feeling ill at ease that Claudia was in a place of drugs and sex traffic, Est had been much relieved at the sight of familiar and beloved Maltby. Claudia was in heaven, overjoyed at the clean freshness of him as much as anything, everyone at the Abbey being dirty and smelling like rutting goats.

Maltby and Claudia had caught up on mutual compliments while Est completed her heroin deal, buying what seemed to her a huge amount of the drug for a nominal price. 100 grains, enough she believed to kill an army, cost little more than a case of good wine.

The package made her feel shaky; its presence inside the bosom of her dress had played on her mind as she'd settled down to a drink with Maltby and Claudia. Some invisible influence seeped through that package and into her heart, slowing the usual pattern of her emotions. Her fascination with it had puzzled her. She'd used the drug before, and although she'd loved its mellow serpentine insinuations, it had not interested her beyond the course of its stay in her body. She'd forgotten heroin easily; there had been no love affair in the offing, as there seemed to be now. She'd obviously changed since fraternising with charismatic Great Beast.

Maltby noticed the change in her. Her cheeks had grown hollow, but that was not the change that worried him. He had been made anxious by a new silence about her. She had not volunteered information, but waited until he'd asked a question and even then she'd often ignored him or turned the conversation to the here and now. She'd chatted about the seedy café, about Palermo, Sicily, but not about the actual goings on at the Abbey, except for a curious remark to the effect that she hadn't painted because of low hygiene levels, a connection he had not been quite able to fathom.

'But what about the work, the Great Beast and his Great Work?' pursued Maltby. Claudia sipped upon a lime cordial and kicked Est nonchalantly under the table, growing bored.

'I watch him mainly. I don't paint. The work of the Abbey progresses. It isn't much of a place yet, although he says we're going to have real walls, real doors and real floors.'

Maltby had asked many similar questions and only got routine information about the structure of the place.

'I mean the metaphysics. Have you engaged your consciousness on any plane other than the mundane?' Maltby drained his espresso.

Est played with the glass handle of her cup with a far away look in her attractive blue eyes. 'Attractive! Why I can't keep my eyes off them,' Maltby thought, unreasonably disgusted with himself as he let the fourth masculine derrière pass without proper appraisal.

'I suppose so,' Est acknowledged.

Maltby was perplexed. 'Come on, let's get the paint and canvas and go on up to this famous Abbey.'

Claudia made a face. 'It's disgusting. That dirty man poohs all over the place and never cleans up after himself.'

'Hush, dear,' Est put her fingers to her lips. 'He'll see for himself soon.'

'Is he coming? Is he coming?' Claudia jumped up pushing her chair back so hard it fell over with a crash that brought all the dark brown eyes in the place upon her. 'Are you coming with us?' She wound her arms round Maltby's neck while the necks swivelled away from them, routinely. She kissed his shaved cheeks and stroked his perfumed hair.

'Yes, I am.'

'Yes, yes! Yes! How long for, how long?'

'That depends on how I get on with this Beast fellow.'

Claudia turned up her nose. 'You'll hate him; he's dirty and he never eats food.'

'Hush, dear.' They'd spoken a little too loudly in a foreign language and Est felt eyes upon them.

'What does he eat then?' Maltby asked her.

'He eats...' Claudia whispered into his ear so Est wouldn't hear.

'No?'

Claudia nodded sagely.

'Whatever it is, I expect it's true,' Est concurred, but her eyes wandered.

Maltby had thought she was probably exhausted and needed to paint. What if it was true? What if Great Beast did tear raw meat with his teeth, from a living goat and sucked warm milk straight from the udder? What if he did these things? And if he did, what else would he do? Would there be anything he wouldn't do?

They had arrived tired at the Abbey. Cheerful voices and soft candlelight came from the Kitchen Shack where preparation for the banquet was well-nigh complete.

3.2 Claudia's Warning

'You weren't exaggerating; this place is a dump,' Maltby confirmed.

Est was joyful in the moonlight, glad of stars and night.

'Good grief, where am I going to sleep?' he worried. The three shacks were as impractical accommodation as the outhouses of a toy farm.

Voices proceeded from the Kitchen Shack, while heads passed to and fro in front of the amber-lit window.

'We all sleep in there.' Est pointed to the Sleeping Shack.

'All together?' Maltby sat down upon his sturdy leather case, his joints cracking. He adjusted his pressed trousers and brushed off some invisible flecks of dust. He wondered how long he'd have to stay in this godforsaken hole before he could persuade Est that she and Claudia had to leave. He chuckled at his perplexity at Abbey life.

'What are you laughing at?' asked Claudia, who had dashed off to the kitchen to beg some tidbits and now returned nibbling a gingerbread star.

'Where do you sleep, fair princess?'

'I'll show you. It's awful and there are *beetles* in the bed.' She took Maltby into the shack and showed him her and Est's bed on one side, made up neatly. Across on the other side were mangled heaps of clothes, ceremonial garments and what not, where Pet, Animal and sometimes Miss Jane slept.

'Vomit sleeps here,' indicated Claudia.

'Vomit?'

'That's her name. Great Beast, who used to be plain Beast, became Great Beast who does Great Work instead of Work. He named Vomit, Vomit. She used to be called Miss Jane when she was my teacher. Vomit. Don't look so disgusted; it always smells like this in here.

'Animal never uses soap; she likes a natural smell, to show her true nature. She says that if someone doesn't want to know you because of your smell, then they're not worth knowing anyway.

'What do you think?' Poised on tiptoe Claudia sniffed his collar. 'You smell a little bit greasy, a bit of perfume; I can smell tobacco too.'

Claudia's charm didn't carry Maltby along as it usually did. 'There's nowhere to wash here, is there?'

'Nowhere to wash, you're right there, for the first point,' replied Claudia in a business-like manner. 'Point two, nowhere to sleep unless you want to sleep with Great Beast over there.' She pointed to the spooky looking Ceremonial

Shack. 'And you never know what he'll do to you.' She opened her eyes wide, so he could see the whites.

'I'll have to risk it.'

'You'll regret it,' she sang, wandering back to the Kitchen Shack. 'Regret it, regret it, regret it! All the girls want babies. They're all going to have Beast babies. You'll regret it!' She raised her voice from inside the kitchen, sticking her head out of the window as Maltby disappeared inside the Ceremonial Shack as if darkness itself was sucking him into its infinite belly.

3.3 Pre-Ritual

'Come on Claudia, you must go to bed now,' Est encouraged.

'Why do you get all the fun?'

'That's not true.'

'It is. Why should I go to bed when I haven't got a bed only a pile of straw full of ants and beetles. And I won't sleep because you'll be making loads of noise having a party.'

'It's not a party, it's a magickal rite.'

'I'm not going to sleep,' insisted Claudia, nevertheless wandering over to her bed. Est had put a bowl of water outside the shack.

'You wash and brush your teeth while I find a light and think of a story to tell you. Have you got any special requests?'

'So long as it isn't a story about Great Beast. I'm fed up with hearing about him and *anyway*, I don't think he's as marvellous as you lot make him out to be,' Claudia sulked. She was tired, nearly nodding off as she drew the brush rhythmically across her teeth.

'Alright, it won't be about Great Beast.'

Est found a small paraffin lantern and set it on a large flat stone she'd hauled into use as a bedside table. She got into her own bed next to Claudia's and pulled a letter out of her dress. It was addressed to Animal; she'd picked it up at the Post Office. It was from someone called Mahoney and it had his name on the back. He had to know her pretty well, to know Animal was here. Est had thought Animal's only friends were Pet, Great Beast and a sister she'd talked about once.

She held the letter up to the light. The paper was thin, with translucent rows of neat black words marching across it with romantically looped consonants. Est intuited that this was a love letter, from man to woman. She placed it carefully on Animal's bedding.

While Claudia finished washing, Est pondered on Great . Beast's earlier words. He'd said that after tonight everything would change. That from tomorrow the Abbey of Love would be a different place; it would throb with efficiency, cleanliness and endeavour focussed in all variety of creative expression.

'Does that mean I'll paint?' she wondered. Painting seemed far away, beyond her current domain.

Claudia cuddled up to her. The voices from the kitchen

sounded happy and relaxed. Est told her daughter a good night story about a bookseller who kept a bookshop full of curious passages and unexpected rooms and would only ever sell a book if he had at least two copies of it, and only then with the greatest reluctance. To buy a book from his shop was to squeeze water from a stone. Neither did he like customers coming and doing what he'd call *poking their noses* around his shop, so gradually customers stopped visiting the shop, stopped opening the books and turning over their old and dusty pages.

Then one day, a young woman walked into the shop.

Claudia's breathing was long and even. She was asleep. Est could return to adult company and the forthcoming ceremonial.

3.4 Divine Guidance

'No, you'll drop it - hold it evenly in the middle - the weight isn't balanced - the bottle's going over.' Est caught it.

They carried the table laid out with the feast to the Ceremonial Shack, amidst much laughter. For his contribution to the endeavour, Great Beast held his alder staff aloft and intoned in Hebrew; he brought forth throaty vibrations of a language he had not been born to.

His chant told of the transference of his Thelemites to divine shells he would create for each of them, kind of conceptual space suits within which each would be endowed with an artificial consciousness modelled upon a higher intelligence. Each member of the Abbey of Thelema at Cefalù would have a new mode of being - a whirling disc with Great Beast's Holy Guardian Angel, Aiwaz, acting as their guide through the universe.

He invoked gods and goddesses, stars and energy

currents in a specific way to accomplish his specific task. At this he was expert, for he was Ipsissimus (greater self) no less, Great Beast.

'Tonight,' he thrilled, 'we shall adore our divinities! Tomorrow we shall rebuild our Abbey!' His erection was consistent and hard, a good omen that the rites would go well.

'Tonight I will endure it all; I will orgasm until my brain bursts. In lustful fever my lechery shall be superb. We shall go to heaven by the debauched power of Great Beast and his harlots.' He raised his staff starwards as the banquet table was finally established in the Ceremonial Shack.

'Babalon, I salute you! Tear off your clothes and daub your body with the signs of lust. Paint your flesh red and gold, declare yourself aroused and ready! Let no cowardly anxiety or hesitation hold back the full pelt of your true nature!'

Great Beast's silhouette was a dark shadow across the face of the moon. His face and lips were purple; huge gleaming gems were clipped to his ears. He entered the Ceremonial Shack. Animal was naked and daubed in red and silver paint in exquisite designs down her spine and across her thighs. The emblem of the Beast was emblazoned between her breasts, her stomach was a riot of serpentine forms.

'Babalon!' He made complex signs in the air with his left hand, the sigils for this important magickal operation.

A wild screeching came from a dark corner the other side

of the banqueting table. Vomit hung upside down from a piece of iron projecting from the wall. Her legs were hooked uncomfortably over the iron, which shifted a little in its rather ancient mortar. In the manner of a bat, she swung and screeched. She was naked, daubed in black and silver stripes. She wore a bat headdress and creepily she seemed exactly like a bat.

Est wore a simple white toga and a gold band around her head; her feet were bare. She held a brass jug in one hand and a wide mouthed goblet or graal in the other. Slowly she poured liquid from the jug into the graal vessel.

Great Beast resumed his Hebrew, saying the magickal words that would transform the simple spring water in the jug into the divine elixir of the gods. The water foamed and spat inside the graal vessel. Bubbles rose from the cup.

Great Beast's high purpose would materialise; he would communicate fantastic, necessary truths to those who came after him. He would preserve ancient knowledge and pass it on, would bust a gut for the cultural dark side. He was indeed laying the foundations for future magick.

Earlier on in the Ceremonial Shack, Maltby had crashed out in the straw behind the altar, exhausted in every conceivable way. He was awakened by Vomit's screeching and several other noises he could not immediately identify.

There was a strange drone in his ears; Maltby swallowed hard to pop them. The drone persisted like the rumble of an enemy aircraft. He was scared; his scalp prickled and his palms oozed sweat. He wiped his hands, first in the straw, which simply stuck to him, then on his trousers and then through his hair, which lifted up and stood in spikes.

Candlelight flickered as it moved around the shack, emanating from a candle held in hands Maltby could not identify. He recognised the voice of the drone; it sent shivers of fear and excitement down his spine.

What were they preparing to do? He was sure that what would be done here could not be done sober in daylight, could only be done drunk, at night.

A flute joined the voice, playing long damp notes, sleazy and fetid. Smouldering incense was swung about in a brass censer and as it swung its bright brass reflected candlelight and flashed metallic spheres around the room. Thick frankincense vapour made his throat constrict and his eyes smart. He tasted Eastern sweetness on his tongue, reminiscent of stimulating oriental twilight.

Fear made him irrational. Spontaneously Maltby jumped up, tore his trousers off and danced around in his socks. The rasping drone penetrated right into his eardrums and sinuses; they buzzed with the sound of breath blown through a comb and paper. The vibration travelled from the inside of his head down into his belly. His arms rose up to the horizontal.

Thus did Maltby participate in the rite, drawn in by the wisdom of Ipsissimus, his irreverent metaphysics and his unshakeable arrogance. Maltby opened his mouth and emitted a long bass note, a bearish growl. His true nature was aroused.

3.5 Ceremony

Animal began the ceremony. She knelt before Great Beast. 'My body is hollow. The sensation of life draining from my limbs is strong. My bodily vices are only possible because of my body. My body dissolves into liquid which pours into this magickal pentagram.

'I am Babalon 156, consort to Great Beast 666. I am whore of the stars and star of all whores.

'I invoke the turquoise lord. Lead us into the past, into ourselves and into your mysteries. Turquoise-masked god, step out from the abysmal forces initiated by Shugal-Choronzon, step out from script and memories and come forth as a living god in our ceremony tonight. Ra-Hoor-Khuit awaken our minds, give us visions, be our vision.

'Grant true sight to our seer, Babalon,' Great Beast requested, 'that we may awaken this modern world to your glory.'

'We open ourselves,' Animal declared in utmost solemnity as Great Beast's lingam penetrated her yoni.

'We open ourselves,' repeated Est, Vomit, Pet and the initially reluctant Maltby, now fascinated and unable to remain aloof.

'We open ourselves.' Animal raised her voice as her neck arched in the preliminary stage of orgasm.

Priest and Priestess performed the rite of sexmagick within the pentagram. The rest of the company were the protectorate, each taking up position on an arm of the star, leaving the apex unoccupied, as a seat is left empty at the sacred table for the uninvited guest.

Aroused, the company observed the act of sexmagick. In religious awe, they hummed, a buzzing hum with vibrating lips. Their humming encouraged the Priestess to secrete the secret elixir for the Priest to suck upon, in order that he might wallow in the totality of divinity that only the vaginal secretions of a Priestess could initiate, secretions engendered through her alchemical magick, the creation of the 16 kalas, the forbidden colours.

Great Beast ejaculated in Animal's yoni with much enthusiasm and satisfaction, as she clung to his rod of sexual power with the concentric muscles of her cunt.

'Suck my nectar. It is unique. It is plentiful,' rasped out Animal in a voice thick with heroin and wine from the ceremonial graal.

'Suck her nectar,' responded the chorus of Est, Pet, Vomit and Maltby, sucking in their lips and hissing the word of power, 'Ixaxaar'.

'Suck my nectar!' commanded Animal, a ritually significant third time.

Great Beast knelt before the Priestess of the ever-returning apocalypse and spoke of his devotion. 'I will suck your nectar because you command me to do so. Whatsoever you command me to do, I will do.

'Open thy thighs,' he entreated humbly. 'Let me see you drip the sacred juice of your kalas, Babalon my whore, whom I adore by duty, nature and Law.'

Great Beast's lips greedily kissed Animal's labia. He sucked the liquid which oozed from her cunt. He dipped his tongue into the rainbow froth of her yoni to drink fulsomely of her heavenly juice.

Then he asked the Priestess to spill the visions from her mind, those given by Ra-Hoor-Khuit, just as she had spilt the sacred fluid, rich with kalas, from her cunt.

'Open your mind, Babalon. Let the god make art within your mind. Be open, be free, be true.'

'Be open, be free, be true,' responded the chorus, thrice.

'Smite me down, if I be unworthy Priest of you. Oh Ra-Hoor-Khuit, raise me up if I be worthy. I entreat you to come amongst us. Descend into our prepared Priestess; fill her with creativity. Give her visions and give her voice to speak of them.' Great Beast made passes to each point of the pentacle. He spat out a drop of sacred cunt juice from his mouth on to his hands and traced the secret sigils that would invoke Ra-Hoor-Khuit. He prayed that this magickal operation would achieve its intended aim, 'To spread the Law of Thelema to the five continents of the world, to bring heavenly approval upon this Priest and Priestess and gold to confirm this approbation.'

Animal as Babalon confirmed:

'I am open, I am free. I put my heart in your hands, oh mighty Ra-Hoor-Khuit. Turn my obedient heart into the material that great souls are made of, transform my emotions into splendid fantasies of the gods.'

'She is open, she is free,' responded the chorus.

'I am open, I am free,' reiterated Animal. 'Ra-Hoor-Khuit, hear me! Work with the shapes of my memory, mould them into creatures of your divine fantasy.

'All powerful!
Merciless!
Terrifying, golden, eagle headed beauty,
More than my love, yet my love
Mortifying in your splendour.'

Animal writhed in ecstasy pulling her labia apart and showing her red swollen genitalia to the gathered company.

'Your Will is supreme,' Great Beast declared in adoration of the god.

'Your Will is supreme,' repeated the chorus.

'Let your Will be my Will.'

'Your Will is his Will. His Will is True Will,' intoned the chorus.

'The seer shall see. The scribe shall record.' Great Beast gestured to Maltby to take up the Great Book which lay upon the altar.

Maltby looked confused. Great Beast clicked his fingers and stared at Maltby fixedly.

'I appoint you scribe. Write.' There was no disobeying that voice. Maltby picked up book and pen and returned to his arm of the pentacle.

Back in England Mama Shag danced in ghostly company around her fire, adding her energy in astral expression of the 93 current to the ritual proceedings, while in Cefalù the seer saw.

'I see a tall turquoise pillar; it is one post of an arch,' Animal intoned. 'I see the other. The archway is the stride of god.' She paused and Great Beast nudged Animal to encourage her to express her vision in its entirety.

'I see hieroglyphics carved upon the pillar,' she obliged.

'What do they look like? Can you describe any?' prompted Beast probing her vagina with three fingers.

'I see an owl and a whirling disc.'

'Good. What else?'

'I see sheaths of grain - a harvest. I see numbers and I see neat channels of water. I see figs and dates, fruit of all kinds. I am in a beautiful garden.'

'Come out of the garden, Babalon. If you play too long in there, you will never get out again,' ordered Beast in a dread tone.

'I was coming out anyway. I didn't like it there; it never rains and I'm so thirsty. Give me a drink.' Great Beast pulled his fingers from out of Animal's cunt with a squelch and handed her the magickal graal cup brimful with drug laced wine. She drained it and asked for more.

'Ra-Hoor-Khuit is here now. He is very hot. I am scratching.'

'Do not feel the heat,' commanded Great Beast.

'Cooler now - still warm. Ra-Hoor-Khuit says the carving upon the pylonic archway is not important. He says we should go through, for then we will be dead but not dead, alive but not alive.' Animal's fingers stretched her throbbing vagina, entered and explored.

'Pass by the archway. Describe Ra-Hoor-Khuit and his intention for us. Is he pleased with us?' continued Beast.

'He is pleased. He fills my mind with vapour, turns my body turquoise. He tells me we need not worry; he will be the father of the future, of our future.

'He will father children tonight, for he can wait no longer. If we wait, he will be too hot and destroy the human host. This is what he communicates.'

'We hear and obey,' returned the chorus and Great Beast.

'We obey and we act.' Animal joined the chorus. Tonight was the night to beget Magickal Children.

Like a ship tossed by wave after storm-wave, the assembled party rode the creative tide of Ra-Hoor-Khuit emanating from Animal in mauve tentacles of light. Animal was beautiful, radiant. The mauve light imploded and turned turquoise as Great Beast entered her yoni. He eased his pulsating staff between the soft caressing folds of her nervously ecstatic hole. After a bevy of triumphant strokes within this familiar territory he withdrew, a moment before ejaculation. He flipped the Priestess over, this easily done as she weighed barely more than a skeleton.

Beast's phallic member dripped. Vomit licked her lips and rushed to intervene before he plunged hilt deep into Animal's anus. Vomit hungrily wrapped her lips round Beast's lingam and licked up his magickal fluid. Then she squealed, for someone had crept up behind her and pierced her anus.

Great Beast laughed throatily. His eyes were hard and metallic. As squealing Vomit released his penis, he fulfilled his intention to sodomise Babalon.

Vomit's squeal sexually stimulated Pet, who enjoyed the sound of a woman in pain. His lingam investigated every crevice of her anus as he held her shoulders tightly with a sinewy hand.

Great Beast withdrew from Babalon's anus. He was saving ejaculation for procreation on this long white night in which Ra-Hoor-Khuit had promised three Magickal Children. He threw his head back and laughed, unhooking a lash from the wall.

'Lick him Vomit, as I lick you,' he commanded and thrashed her across the stomach.

His command was momentarily unclear to her as her body steamed with devilish sexual heat, insatiable. Great Beast brought the lash down again, upon the loose flesh of her stomach. Her eyes boggled as she perceived his meaning. She was to lick Pet's prick clean after it had been in her anus. She grovelled before Beast on the hard stone floor, burying her head in the soiled straw and protesting against his command.

Great Beast commanded Pet with a movement of his fingers and Pet stripped Vomit of what remained of her robes. Her great buttocks were revealed quivering in the candlelight. Pet, acting under orders, dripped hot candle wax on to these buttocks.

Vomit squealed as she lay flat on the straw, clenching and unclenching her buttocks furiously in mounting orgasm. She flipped on to her back and opened her thighs and the she lifted her torso from the ground.

'Shag me,' she screamed. 'Shag me! Somebody shag me!'

Around her she saw still white faces but what was huge and towering to her were the two lingams, no, three. Maltby had come to watch too and had uncovered his rod of power. She salivated and screamed again.

'Shag me, shag me!'

With a small hand gesture Great Beast commanded Pet who obediently straddled her, his penis against her lips.

Greedily she sucked it into her mouth, pushing back the foreskin, not minding now that she licked at her own shit.

Great Beast held the cup up to Maltby's mouth. Maltby

drained the graal and looked into Great Beast's hard vital eyes for assent, which was given. Maltby crouched over Vomit's cunt, getting in there, getting up there and shagging her. As his grinding intensified, Pet withdrew his sticky prick from her mouth to let her enjoy the fuck she had begged for.

Her breasts wobbled, her nipples were hard. The company gathered around the copulating couple and hummed with half closed eyes. They observed the length of his shaft as he withdrew, her cunt holding him firm all the while. They looked at her pink and stretchy insides trying to turn inside out to hold on to him. They watched while he came up her, as her back arched and her mouth opened in silent scream after silent scream, to complete the act of magickal copulation upon a rustic floor.

Pet, Great Beast and Babalon (Animal), concentrated on this act of coitus, lips abuzz as they watched Maltby's building climax. His face was marked with the red hot spots of orgasm.

He climaxed with a roar, in an act of magickal procreation that brought Ra-Hoor-Khuit into Maltby's novice body. Est watched from the doorway. She had left the ceremony when Vomit had squealed under sodomy, sure the bloodcurdling sound would have woken Claudia and determined now that they had to leave this place - get away from endless cleaning, cooking and shagging (or in her case, voyeurism) to paint again.

The air in the Sleeping Shack had been warm, full of the

steady breath of Claudia, still asleep. 'Thank god.' Est was relieved. A full moon shone down as she returned slowly to the ceremony. Contemplatively, she chewed on a crust of dry bread.

From the doorway she watched Maltby's ecstasy with some jealous hot throbbing in her cunt. This place and these people attracted her as much as they repelled her. Still, for Claudia's sake she had to go back to Paris, she supposed, to check the sales of her paintings. She hoped to have enough money to pay for Claudia's education.

She found a peach in her pocket and took a bite. First it was furry, then juicy. She laughed faintly to herself.

Post orgasm Maltby was stunned and embarrassed at his nakedness. He rummaged around for a garment to wrap around himself and collided with the altar knocking the candle over, which spluttered and was extinguished in a puddle of spilt wine. The place was now dark but for a soft ray of moonlight, which slipped idly past Est and across the straw where Vomit lay. It gently illuminated her bosom and her robe which lay, torn, beside her.

Idly the hardcore Thelemite group did their norm. Great Beast penetrated Babalon's cunt while Pet penetrated Great Beast's anus. Laconically they rocked together as moonlight passed across Babalon's belly and inspired Great Beast. Ra-Hoor-Khuit had entered him and he would impregnate Babalon. He roared out arcane words and Est flinched, hiding herself away more completely.

Maltby scurried out of the stable, clutching garments to his chest, in a self-protective gesture. Vomit lay sleeping, unconscious, head turned to one side. A small pool of semen seeped out of her yoni, wetting her thighs.

Est caught Maltby's shoulder as he left, their eyes met. 'We've got to go,' she mouthed. Maltby nodded. 'Now,' she whispered. He nodded again, thinking most that he needed to wash before putting his clothes on.

'We haven't time,' Est answered his thoughts. As they went together to the Sleeping Shack, they paused outside so as not to disturb Claudia. Weird grunting continued from the Ceremonial Shack.

The noises persuaded Maltby that there was no time for washing, or any type of delay. Soon Great Beast would have finished his business. He might turn over and sleep quietly or he might step out to chant to the dawn. They didn't want to meet him before leaving, didn't want to give him the chance to do some magick and exert his charismatic hold over them so they would be unable to leave.

Dawn came lending all a hazy grey demeanour. In the grey, they found Maltby's suitcase, tossed to one side in the scrub behind the shack. This they packed with their bare necessities. Now to wake Claudia and scarper.

The sound of the sea below was enervating and a light moist breeze came off the sea. Maltby and Est were leaden-eyed. She wore neat navy slacks and a clean white shirt - chic bohemian, the only woman in trousers on the island.

He was altogether more haywire. From where they stood in the doorway to the shack they could hear Claudia's even breathing. They looked round sharply as Great Beast appeared in naked whiteness with flabby bits hanging hairless from his symmetrical skeleton. They reached for each other's hand in an impulse of pure fear and entwined fingers around fingers for reassurance.

Befuddled Great Beast had not come to question or summon them or demand money. He pissed profusely on to the ground where his urine steamed. His lackadaisical co-ordination was by courtesy of heroin and cocaine. There were no birds singing in his head that morning.

Est tugged Maltby's arm and led him up the rocky hill behind the shacks to a small grassy meadow, where they could take one last look at the sea. The atmosphere of the Abbey, the appearance of Great Beast and their conspiratorial togetherness combined with the beauty of the morning and it became suddenly the obvious thing to do to throw their clothes off and make love, as Ra-Hoor-Khuit was their witness.

Their act of copulation surprised them. They had never made love before. It was body against body, joy, lots of air and a sensation of speed, of moving away from Earth towards red fire and the abstract land of origin.

As orgasm began to move within them, the sweat on Maltby's back collected in the palm of Est's hand and reminded her that this fellow was no god, he was her friend.

Yet here they were, abandoning themselves in accordance to the Will of Ipsissimus, Great Beast, without inhibition or consideration outside the power of his Will.

A slothfully resinous voice penetrated their post-coital vulnerability. Beast had dragged himself up here for his regular morning salutation to the gods.

'All you do, all you are, only exists within my Will.' His words slurred together.

'Love is the Law,' he recited.

'Love under Will,' they rejoined.

Great Beast impatiently gestured them away. Hurriedly, they gathered their clothes and scuttled down the rocks.

'We must go,' said Est, 'before anything else happens.'

Maltby smiled, not participating in her sense of urgency. 'That's what you said before.' He reached for her hand.

'I think not,' she snapped. 'Forget it. This didn't happen. We were not here. We are not here.'

'It was Ra-Hoor-Khuit?'

'Yes, it was. I just want to get back to normal.'

Back in the Sleeping Shack, Est buckled on Claudia's sandals, smoothed down her hair and told her about the long journey ahead of them.

'Now?' asked Claudia sleepily.

'Yes, now, my love.'

'Have you booked the boat?'

Est laughed. Her daughter was so practical and thoughtful.

'No... if there are no places for us on board, we can stay in town until the next boat.'

'I'm glad we're going. Can we go back to Paris?'

'Yes, we're going to Paris and I expect you can go back to school.'

'I'm so glad. I'm so glad. I hate that Beast. He makes me sick. He gives me the creeps and Animal is getting as bad as him. She stinks. Her hair is full of lumps of dirt and her teeth are black and falling out.'

Est stroked her hair. 'We're going now, back to civilisation.' She looked at Maltby, his cream slacks stained and creased, his mid-blue shirt half in and half out of his trousers, his jacket crushed. He looked wasted, his lips drooped and stubble peppered his chin. It was the expression in his eye that worried her most, he seemed radically changed and he'd only arrived yesterday.

The expression in his eye would take more than a couple of hours grooming to clean up. It was crazier than an insane monkey. Where was her reliable art dealer, the one who had come to rescue her?

They walked down the rough track to the village where the Thelemites got their basic food supplies. Maltby hummed and swung the suitcase merrily, entirely unconcerned that two of his shirt buttons were undone and his hair was stuck up scarecrow-like. Claudia was wary of him. She had moved to the side of Est furthest from Maltby and furtively gave him small worried glances. Maltby did not notice Claudia's behaviour, he who was usually sensitive and attentive to her moods.

'Est?'

'Yes Claudia?'

'Est?'

'I said, "yes" darling.'

'Est?'

'What is it Claudia? Are you worried about something?'

'Well sort of, not *something* exactly.'

'Someone then?' queried Est, glad to be filling this difficult time of escape with conversation.

'Yes, that's right. I am worried about him.' She lowered her voice, but needn't have bothered, Maltby was oblivious.

'So am I,' concurred Est.

'Has he got to him?' Claudia drew closer to Est and hissed through her teeth.

'I wouldn't be surprised,' Est replied. 'His character is rather weak in many ways. I wouldn't worry too much. I'd be more worried if he had a strong character. Strong people always take so much longer to recover from injury. The humiliation of realising their imperfections affects them profoundly. After a bit of time in our company away from this place and *certain* people he'll soon be fine.' They continued their walk in silence.

'There's the old donkey. Do you think he'll take us into town?' Claudia asked. Est stroked their useful friend's hairy ears.

'I hope so,' she said. 'Give him a lump of sugar and I'm sure he will.'

So, for not much more than the cost of a lump of sugar they travelled from village to town, from town to port and from port to city. Maltby came along too, although he was hardly able to contribute to conversation or notice his surroundings. Est managed to keep his hair brushed and his face, hands and neck washed; but as for his feet and his penis, Ra-Hoor-Khuit only knew when they would next see soap and water.

They arrived in Paris, home, with one imbecile art dealer, one undernourished ego and one child in need of schooling. Step one was to get rooms habitable, step two to find out how the paintings had been selling.

'Surprising really,' thought Est, as she busied herself around the gloomy basement, 'how small a portion of time has passed since we were last here. I never believed we'd return, yet here we are.'

'Claudia!' she called. 'Tea's ready. Wash your hands, won't you? Claudia!'

'I'm coming, I'm just taking Maltby a glass of water.'

Poor Maltby! Abed with an illness of the mind.

∴four

4.1 Where is Maltby?

On their fourth morning back in Paris, Est woke early, foggy with all sorts of organisational necessities. The business of life pressed upon her bladder, not such a romantic feeling, a full bladder. She stumbled in the early morning gloom, hand on three door handles before she reached their outside WC, hair messy and soul awry. 'It must be him,' she said to herself; a vivid picture of Beast's head laughing within her own head swamped her and she was awash with nausea.

'Est are you alright? What are you doing in there?'
Claudia called.

Claudia tried the door which opened, for Est only
occasionally locked it. Inside the smallest room it was
gloomy.

'You've got bare feet,' Est noticed. Claudia was shivering.
'Go back inside. I've just woken, that's all.' Claudia
hesitated on the threshold.

'Is it school today?'

'Not yet, next week. Go on. I need a few minutes alone.'

Dreams rushed through Est, as the cold stone floor
chilled her feet. The city smelt musty, yet of honey too and
testosterone, a rich aroma of much activity.

Images surged through her mind, relating to many
remembered dreams - landscapes she invented, edited and
explored. She was walking through a burnt wood. Ash
puffed up from the ground with each one of her light steps,
as if she weighed nothing and earth was all dust.

She became anxious. Why was the wood burnt? Why was
there a wood here at all? She remembered this spot as a
green field with a view of a castle by the sea. The sea
appeared as a shiny grey triangle, a telescopic view through
the half-closed eyes of a sleeping predator. She was the
predator, a falcon. Ahead of her were carefully planned
water gardens, formal flowerbeds and an amusing
arrangement of fountains and statues. Moss grew inbetween
paving stones.

When she'd dreamed this garden before, she'd always walked towards the sea, yet never reached it. Now she walked away from the sea. At the bottom of the sloping field, she saw a team of workers, digging. One sturdy figure signalled to her but his signals meant nothing to her.

At her feet four great orange balls protruded through distressed concrete. She turned one of the balls over with her foot; it rolled to one side, revealing a network of underground passageways. It was an ants' nest and these orange balls were gigantic ant eggs.

*   *   *

Half an hour later Est's mind had cleared. She clonked around in the kitchen preparing hot drinks. She had already spent half an hour lighting the stove. Luckily the fire was drawing well that morning.

'What do you want for breakfast?' No reply. Claudia was playing, talking to herself.

Est, louder. 'Would you like an egg for breakfast?'

'My usual,' answered Claudia.

'Egg on toast?'

'Yes, my usual. Are we going to see Maltby today?'

'I shouldn't think so.'

'Why not? I want to see him. Why haven't we seen him since we got back?'

'Well darling, we haven't been back very long.' Est

cracked two eggs into a bowl and beat them with an ancient fork, its silver plate peeling away. The kettle began to hiss.

'We used to see him every day.'

'Did we?'

'You know we did. Can't we see him today?'

'We'll talk about him after breakfast. Okay?'

'If you say so,' Claudia huffed. 'I don't want to see that Beast again, whatever you say.'

'I shouldn't think we'll see him again. I don't think our paths will cross.'

'Good.'

They ate eggs on toast with milky tea, Claudia looked at Est from time to time with a cocked head, wondering what she was hiding.

*   *   *

Since returning to Paris, Est had also returned to painting, slipping into her old habits as comfortably as Claudia slipped into her solitary games.

Est delineated her mental landscape on canvas. 'I am undermined. How can I continue now the object of my search has been revealed as decadent and chaotic?'

A bare canvas was never empty to her; it always spoke of possibilities of colour, texture and symbolic association. Today, translucency, perspective and space were everything:

these to be expressed in colour in a particular way, to pierce through ordinary conceptual associations of time and space.

She sketched first with brown pastels, then with some red. Soon she reached for paint and brush, impatient with the tools that came between her and the transmission of inspiration.

Creativity was a way of life to her. She imbibed only what would contribute to her art. Several portraits of Great Beast were propped against the wall, all dark and Hispanic for no reason Est could consciously define. She had depicted Great Beast as a man of the inferno, in red and black, large hat set at a slant with only one eye visible.

As she applied light blue to an area of stricken forest, the air behind her quivered. Her back became hot and a voice joined the sensation of hot distorted air.

'Est,' it was Stritch's voice. 'Est.'

His voice excited her beyond measure. She drank a glass of water to compose herself. A *come to me* voice, a *find me* voice. A voice that slipped between her white clothes and her skin. 'Est.'

It was as if he had told her he loved her and touched her heart and her skin and found her soul. She remembered making love with him. Her teeth chattered loudly. The memory was too acute, too close to her, worse than pain because unlike pain, it could not be borne. It was deep memory incarnate.

'Est, what are you painting? Not the horrid old GB

again?' Claudia wandered in from where she had been cutting out paper dolls in her bedroom, wishing she had a clever friend to play cat's cradle with. Even hopping would be more fun if you had someone to do it with.

'It isn't GB, it's who I thought GB might be before I met him.' Est told her daughter.

'It doesn't look like a person. Or...' Claudia paused, she was used to abstract pictures of people. 'Or as if it has anything to do with people. It looks like how day would look like if it came at night. A different idea of day that runs at a different speed from ours.'

'I see what you mean. Did you hear another voice?' asked Est.

'Why?'

'Only asking.' They both assessed the light blue upon the canvas, with a little defining khaki.

'If you're only asking I will tell you I did. Have you got someone hidden in the cupboard?' Claudia opened doors and slammed them shut. 'I hate this place,' she continued. 'The air in here is always still, as if nothing will ever move and nothing will ever change, whatever masterpieces you paint. When are we leaving? When am I going to school? When are we going to see Maltby again?'

Est had been wondering when she'd bring that up again. Becoming a bit of an old chestnut was the subject of Maltby. Claudia had grown up so much, school would be hard for her after this erratic life.

'Let's go out to lunch,' she said decisively. Est put her brushes in jars of turpentine she kept on the chipped kitchen shelf. 'We can talk everything over like civilised people. I'll tell you about Maltby. Wash your face.'

'I know, brush my hair, wash my hands, put my shoes and stockings on.'

'And your hat,' added Est.

'And my hat.'

Both suddenly paused in the pleasant business of getting ready to go out. Their faces were pale and drawn in the musky basement, as they listened intently.

'Est, Est.' A *come to me* voice, Stritch's voice.

'Who's that?' Claudia was afraid, she listened again for the agonised whisper. 'Who is that?' Claudia grasped her mother's clothing and shook her. 'Tell me who it is?' Claudia's panic was tangible.

'It's alright, love,' soothed Est.

'It wasn't alright, it was horrible. Get it away from me. It's a ghost,' she sobbed, hugging her mother. 'I want to leave this place. Only horrible things have happened since we came here. I want to leave this place and never never come back. I want Maltby. Where is he? What has that Great Beast done to him?'

'Hush, it's alright. It's the voice of a friend,' Est soothed. 'Come, put your hat on. Let's have lunch. You must be ravenous. We don't need to ever come back here if you feel that strongly about it.'

'I *do*. Where is Maltby? Tell me now.'

'He's alright,' but Est's voice was unsure. 'Come on, let's go. I'll tell you outside.'

Stritch's voice had unsettled Est and she was wary of communicating her worries to Claudia. She needed to maintain the protective barriers around Claudia that meant whatever the circumstances they found themselves in, the integrity of Claudia's childhood would be preserved. Est was most worried about poor dear Maltby. She locked the door behind her, putting Claudia's hat on and then her own. She could at least rely on the security of hats, if not of feelings.

'How can I tell her about Maltby? How can I not tell her?' Est thought on their way to the café, incidentally, the same café where they often used to meet Maltby and where Mahoney drank at night.

In spite of minestrone soup, Claudia's fear was unabated. She still felt the presence of a ghost and every minute expected the invisible entity to draw up a chair at the table with them. Claudia couldn't keep her eyes off Est, for reassurance. Est was uneasy too, not so much about the unseen Stritch; he didn't trouble her. Stritch had had an ethereal quality while alive and for her, death had not changed him much, only they couldn't have sex. Reluctantly she forced her mind away from the favourite subject of recalling his body in minutest pictorial detail. She loved to remember the opera of their emotions in colour, form and movement.

Even in summer it was comforting to sip soup.

'Do you like the soup?' she asked Claudia, as an entrée to a difficult subject. Claudia understood this. She had a perception not taught in schools.

'You know I like the soup.'

'But what you want to know is…?' interrupted Est.

'What I really want to know,' resumed Claudia, wriggling her toes, 'is about the ghost. Who is he?'

'Ghost?' Est was taken back, she took Stritch's presence for granted. She thought Claudia was thinking about Maltby.

'What ghost? Do you seriously not know?' Claudia was astounded. 'The one that keeps saying, "Est, Est, Est." in a creepy voice. Has it got anything to do with the GB?'

'I suppose he has, indirectly.'

'You're not going to say, "We'll talk about it later"?'

This was the tomorrow that never came. 'I'll tell you about everything and hope it won't overwhelm you to the point where you won't be able to go to school, in what?' Est calculated. 'Three days' time. Tomorrow we'll sort out your uniform.'

'Don't talk about that,' pleaded Claudia, too loudly. A few heads turned to look at les Anglais.

'All right. Maltby first. When we came back from Cefalù?, before we even came here, do you remember we went to see an old friend of mine?'

'Yes,' Claudia listened intently.

'And left Maltby with him. You were very tired. You don't remember? Do you remember how strangely Maltby was behaving from the moment we left the Abbey?'

'Abbey! Huh!'

'Come on Claudia. I'm trying to tell you about Maltby. Please, it's important.'

'I know it's important. Sometimes I think *you* don't think he's important.'

'Will you hear what I have to say?' Est terminally impatient. Claudia sensed this and used the power it gave her.

'I'll listen but not until you promise me we'll never go back home.'

'I'll have to pick up my work.'

'As long as I don't have to go,' pursued Claudia.

'You don't have to go; we can stay in a hotel tonight if you like and buy whatever we need, if you feel that strongly about it.'

'There's a ghost there.' Claudia picked up her soup spoon, satisfied.

'Maybe the ghost will follow us,' suggested Est.

'Are we rich?' Claudia ignored that last statement. It wasn't only because of the ghost she didn't want to go back there. She'd seen a face at the window and she was sure Est had seen it too.

'Quite rich. Everyone loves my paintings and it's all thanks to Maltby's work.' From the middle of nowhere, a tear drifted into her eye. 'Do you remember how strangely he was behaving?' Meaning Maltby.

'He wouldn't look at me and didn't listen to what I said,' Claudia remembered.

'Yes, and he got worse. He stopped being able to feed or dress himself. I took him to a doctor who sent him to a sort of hospital. I don't know if he'll get better. He's had some kind of breakdown. We're not allowed to see him in this hospital, or nursing home, until he's settled in. Even then, I don't want you to go until I've seen him myself.'

Claudia was amazed. Maltby had always been reliable and predictable. 'Is he crazy forever?'

Est was relieved to laugh. 'I don't know. I think he'll get better. Great Beast and his revolutionary ideas blew his mind.'

'Like a cannon. Boom! But he's not dead?'

'Far from it.'

'Let's find somewhere fabulous to live,' Est continued. 'How about England?' An impulsive suggestion.

'England! What about school?'

'You haven't started yet. I think we should go to England.'

'To stay?'

'For a while. Come on. Do you want to finish that lemon ice before we go?' Claudia shook her head and pushed the small bowl of mostly melted sweet water ice away from her. 'I feel a bit sick.'

'Excitement. Come on. Let's go find a fabulous suite in a fabulous hotel and see how the other half live.'

Hand in hand they promenaded down the street, all things considered, feeling pretty good. Would they have felt so good if they had known that the face at their window, the one they both knew about but didn't want to talk about, watched them now? A face worn out from unfulfilled desire.

4.2 The Watcher

Mahoney's great want, his tremendous love for Animal had not gone away. It had grown in absence, exponentionally. It was he who watched Claudia and Est. He clung to them as his only connection with her, with Animal, for he had seen Animal and Claudia together in the same café, all those months ago before they had left for Cefalù.

Mahoney had meantime been wandering and sleeping rough. His intention had been to live close to nature and write verse of eternal value, encompassing great truths and exquisite emotion, emotion brought into focus by solitude - this was the nature of his true love for Animal.

His intention had been worthy, but he did not have the inner strength to keep aloof from lust, a lust that spread like wildfire when catalysed by powerful Great Beast. It burnt out steadiness of purpose and sensible ideas as easily as a forest fire crackled through pine trees in a drought. Lust ravished Mahoney's personality. He had turned wild under the influence of Great Beast.

He'd been sleeping in bushes, living on berries and raw rabbit flesh as if he'd forgotten that Prometheus had brought fire from the gods to man. He strangled rabbits with his bare hands, plunged his teeth into the jugular and while the rabbit still twitched in its death throes, he drank the blood, sucked the blood as its flow eased as the small heart ceased to beat.

The wild man in him took over his personality. His sense of smell improved until he could distinguish human individuals by their distinctive odour. He hid from humans; he no longer thought of himself as one of them, for they smelt bad to him. He was a hound knowing the ways of man, sharing many habits with man, but he did not feel himself to be one of them.

Wild, regressed, Mahoney thought of himself as more than a man. He had become more expert at *being*, within Great Beast's definition of what it was to be, than other men. He had become sensually expert, also, alert and exact in smell, taste, hearing, sight and touch. He could stalk Animal, whom he wanted as mate, without consideration for anything but his male need for her. It grew within him like a black hole, becoming his only reference point, his only motive.

In his Animal-mad wanderings he followed Est and Claudia in Paris, tracking their every move with a predator's prowess.

4.3 Poor Maltby

Maltby was abed tormented and illogical. Est visited him at the lakeside sanatorium, but he did not recognise her. She promised to visit again soon and paid the bill. She had plenty of money. What had once seemed so hard, liaising with an art dealer, she now found easy. A successful and money-generating painter was treated with sycophantic respect be she male or female. However, the Parisian fawning and partying was a pressure she fled from. Her priority was the close company she kept with ghostly Stritch and the transmutation of their love to canvas.

Sadly, however, she was frequently distracted from her work by hoards of critics and amateur painters seeking artistic advice commingled with the occasional businessman after a painter for a mistress. How could she nourish her beloved dead Stritch, incubate him within the warm environs of her living palpitating heart when a hoard of cultural scavengers pressed in upon her physical and psychic resources? Especially now, when on Claudia's insistence, she'd moved from her familiar studio to a hotel suite. In spite of having plenty of money she resented the expense.

Claudia had become clingy and refused to go back to school. Claudia was freaked out by the wild behaviour of her one time teacher, Miss Jane, now known as Vomit. Est did not think that a life hanging around a painter's overalls was a healthy one for a 12 year old. Claudia needed some life and friends of her own.

With these considerations in mind, she thought ever more frequently of Mama Shag's spacious and romantic country home. At *Ridelands* she could paint and Claudia could attend school. Their needs would be accommodated.

∴ five

5.1 Addict in the Straw

Meanwhile, back at the Abbey Est, Claudia and Maltby were hardly missed by the hardcore Thelemites. Their maxim, *Do what thou wilt shall be the whole of the Law*, encouraged spontaneity and Free Will (read unpredictable behaviour).

On the third day of Est's absence, as the contents of the gourmet hamper dwindled, Animal began to look out for Est leading a donkey laden with provisions.

Great Beast rolled over in the straw and called for his cup.

'Wine! Damn you, woman! Burgundy! Animal!' he roared. 'What is this stench? Where is that nameless hussy who wouldn't shag?' Animal returned from her look-out post and crouched barefoot in the soiled straw, her knees slightly parted. The aroma of her cunt wafted from her and soothed Great Beast.

'My Animal, wine.' She poured him the local red from a dark green unlabelled bottle.

'Pah! What is this filth! Yesterday, no heroin. Today horsepiss! Whore woman, you bring me horsepiss and try and cover my finely attuned senses with the smell of your cunt. Don't tell me! The lady who does not shag has left and with her she has taken the ability to telegraph for money.' Great Beast paused, tired by the effort of roaring. Anger could not get a hold on him in the way it use, could not rouse him from vile heroin sickness.

Est had often gone on foraging adventures to Palermo. She'd sent telegraphs to individuals suggested by GB, for his path had crossed with many like minds and some were willing to help sustain the Great Work. Funds had consequently trickled in.

GB lay back upon a stained crimson velvet cushion and threw an arm out, knocking over the offending Sicilian wine.

'Animal, see what heroin is doing to me. My fingers, my belly and my jowls swell. My mind rocks upon the seesaw of transient influence. It has diluted my immortal resources.

Anubis stares into my face now. See how the dog head denies my entreaty.

'I rave.' He regarded Animal beseechingly.

'Lick me clean, my faithful, dutiful whore. Cleanse my face of disaster. I am no hero, no saint.' He held his bloated white face up to her. It gleamed in the light from the doorway. 'I defined all strata of humanity; I separated myself from the natural flow of my generation. I transected the past with my magickally trained mind and from there I found the grimoires holding the keys to propel me into the future at reality-defying speeds.

'I need the heroin, don't you understand, Animal? I need it.' She licked his earlobe. He held out his fingers for her tongue's attention. 'I need the heroin to slow down, heroin is my brake, cocaine my ignition.' He snorted a large pinch of heroin and another for the other nostril.

His chest heaved, taking in much needed oxygen. 'It seems heroin has a stronger Will than I.' He couldn't relax enough to breathe freely without the drug. It held in abeyance the silk worms spinning their cocoons within his respiratory system.

His mind would spin ever faster. Its revolutionary motion was the drug calling to him, asserting itself upon his Will. He felt impelled to call his Thelemites to attend to him and give him heroin. Only then would his mind stop spinning and the breath come back into his body. His asthma was debilitating.

'Get Vomit to cable for money.' His pin prick pupils pierced Animal. She scurried away obediently to find Vomit.

Resignedly Great Beast took three more large doses of heroin in each nostril. He needed to write in his journal and read the post, needed to move his body out of this hovel. He surveyed the scene in great hopelessness. They'd had great plans to rebuild their Abbey. They had whitewashed the rough plaster and he'd painted scenes of revelry upon them, but these were cracking, the plaster crumbling. In spite of everything, he obstinately clung to his identity as a distorted double-take of an English gentleman.

In self assessment GB did not see the distortion. Although he operated outside Christianity, he still considered himself a true gentleman.

Great Beast cringed within his skin. 'Love is the Law,' he murmured weakly, 'Love under Will.' The image of Ra-Hoor-Khuit came before his mind and he breathed freely, assured by the god that there was money coming to him. He could rise today and be nourished. He would be able to travel from his Abbey and write a compelling book of his intriguing life. He would get gold for Ra-Hoor-Khuit was with him.

5.2 Orders are Orders

Animal was physically functioning but talking gibberish and had very little appetite. Pet lay sweating in the sleeping quarters, semi-conscious, waking only to drink. So that left Vomit (Miss Jane), who had become obsessed with . preparing food, particularly pasta with a sauce made of anything soft and vegetable she could find.

Compulsively she cooked this sauce in a big pot over an open fire in the Kitchen Shack. She found the stove too whimsical to manage. The smoke went any which way, filling the room and her eyes, before meandering out of door and window. She had a dirty rag strung around her thick waist; her breasts swayed upon her chest like living entities existing separately from the rest of her body.

She sang as she stirred her pot, old lullabies mainly, with an occasional sea shanty thrown in, when a quick and vigorous mood came upon her, for instance when she served up bowls of her unique gruel and offered them round to her fellow Thelemites. Carefully, she would leave a bowl beside a failing Pet. A row of such bowls lay ranged beside him, untouched.

Vomit ate a lot of pasta and got daily fatter.

Today though was different, for Great Beast was motivated by the feeling for gold. He had a strong and sure knowledge that gold would come, would be waiting for him at the Post Office in Palermo and would lead to a replenished supply of heroin. He would then be able to continue his Great Work of ritual and writing.

This *day* as he called it, the *day* between the Great Ritual for begetting Magickal Children and the gold to nurture them in the image of Ra-Hoor-Khuit, this day without heroin, had lasted five periods of light and dark.

Vomit was quite relieved when Animal called her to audience with Great Beast. It was a great effort for Great Beast to prop himself up on one elbow and for his flabby jowls to lift his jaw into motion. 'Go to Palermo to get gold,' he languidly ordered.

He handed her the documents necessary to cash money orders in his name and instructed Animal to prepare the priestess, Vomit, in ceremonial robes for her sacred mission to the city. No mean feat, for Vomit was a mess.

GB sank back, his eyes darted hither and thither, his wrists and knees twitched with the effort of the slightest movement. He sweated profusely and suffered. A jumbled mixture of words from the twenty one languages with which he was familiar, rotated in his brain, as if they too wished to be sweated out of his system, if only they could find a point of exit.

Absence of heroin was torture. He imagined the opium poppy's brightly coloured purple and red petals fringed with black. He felt himself to be a vulture flying over a field of opium poppies, their black eyes staring at him, to the backdrop of a poppy coloured sunset vibrating with serene promises. He dived down to the field and like a nectar-feeding bat, stuck his tongue deep into a blossom, *papaver sominferum* which extravagantly informed him of true bliss.

Animal's hands twisted together and she shivered with the pressure of responsibility to prepare the Priestess, Vomit. She was also jealous that she hadn't been chosen for this sacred role. Animal was the essence of jealousy and lust, for little else is the Whore of Babalon.

Vomit squealed like a baboon as Animal pulled her by the hand away from her cooking pot. Animal coughed with the smoke but Vomit was more affected by the brilliant sun. She cowered and shaded her eyes. Like a hippopotamus Vomit pulled away from Animal's determined grip but Animal held on to her. Vomit at last acquiesced to her Will. Animal handed her the letter of sacred duties written by Great Beast, bearing his magickal seal, the kind of document one simply did not disobey. The letter smelt of his personal cologne and his favourite perique tobacco.

'Do what thou wilt shall be the whole of the Law,' he began under his seal. 'As Priestess of Isis, Mother of Horus (crowned and conquering child), you will embark upon a sacred journey to the great city [Palermo] where you will collect gold that Ra-Hoor-Khuit has allocated to his emissaries on earth. Gold, to allow the process of revealing to be continued.

'Draw off your primitive skin and wear the elegant veil of woman of knowledge, woman of Thebes, woman of Babalon, pregnant whore you are.' The letter ended with the motto *Love is the Law, Love under Will,* followed by Great Beast's seal of a seven pointed star of Babalon superimposed with a phallus. Vomit casually pouted and blew Animal a kiss, knowing the gesture would excite her.

Animal moved closer to meet her lips. They opened their mouths and felt each other's lips. Their hearts fluttered happily.

'What are you two doing?' Great Beast boomed from across the yard. He'd dragged himself up to get a bottle of wine and evacuate his bowels.

'Get on with your jobs. Stop this horrible Sapphic behaviour. Mere fiddling, mere fiddling.' His voice trailed off effeminately.

The girls giggled in the manner of Shakespearian witches, their stomachs clenched in hunger.

5.3 Friends

'Your back is engrained with dirt and you have sores upon your buttocks. Poor darling!'

Vomit scrubbed Animal with an oval stone. The cold mountain stream here opened out into a small pool which reached up to their knees.

Animal's skin was white, threaded with veins and half-healed whip marks. There were numerous scabs, particularly at the back of her neck where dried blood plastered her hair to the mildly suppurating wounds.

Vomit washed the ceremonial paint from between her thighs, rubbed the remains of hieroglyphics from her belly and scrubbed at the Celtic lattice work encircling her navel. Between her breasts were the obstinate black marks forming the mark of Great Beast. This she could not wash away, for this was a tattoo.

Animal turned this way, bent that, as Vomit instructed. She was not gibbering but wasn't exactly talking either.

'Please talk to me,' pleaded Vomit. 'Can't we be friends again. We're here together, let's talk.'

Animal sat on a rock, forlorn, while Vomit squatted in the water and washed each of Animal's toes carefully, doing the best she could to clean the caked grime out with a twig. 'I wish I had a small pair of scissors, to cut your nails. Silver needlework scissors, about so big.' Animal's nails were discoloured, cracked at their tips and ridged due to non-fatal malnutrition. For this reason too, she had mouth ulcers.

Animal pushed her knotted hair behind her ears. She was impelled by a throbbing rhythm more powerful than the burble of the stream. She took Vomit by the hand and pulled insistently.

'All right, I'll come with you,' Vomit acquiesced, 'on one condition, that you say, "come with me" and say it nicely too.' She finished on a teacherly note.

'Come,' said Animal, 'with' and pointed to herself, her hazel eyes, wide and girlish. Too girlish in Vomit's estimation, hardly sane and competent. 'And what, I wonder,' she said to herself, 'is to become of this one when Great Beast has used her up with his demands?' She felt a wave of moral revulsion at Great Beast's philosophy. Forgotten details of pleasant family life came to the surface of her thoughts.

'The new order will have to progress without me,' Vomit asserted. She held Animal's hand and followed her down to the sea, whither Animal was frequently drawn.

They splashed in waves that washed upon the small beach bordered closely by rocks. Vomit's bare feet bled. 'Here we are splashing in the sea in the most beautiful place in the world, two ladies both probably pregnant, probably by the same man, both mad with desire for him, half dependent (or more) on his drugs, eager for his wisdom. His Magick!' Vomit shouted.

Salt foam ran between her fingers. She raised her head to the sun; colour flooded into her eyes, formless and wise like only nature could be when stripped of preconceived definition. That is what Great Beast had done for her, opened her to the pure colour of the universe and given her the ability to see/feel/live in an intense moment of unforgettable experience. She would not have exchanged the gifts of these scattered moments for the comfort and contentment of any sober life.

'Ravishing,' she called. 'I am ravished.' She threw herself, naturally naked, into the waves saying quietly to herself, 'I'll still have to be off, have to go. Can't give birth, that's if I am pregnant, in the appalling squalor of the Abbey.'

Animal laughed aloud, though Vomit thought her laugh always sounded like the empty echo of one trapped by an enchantment. It was the laughter of one who wished so badly, madly to live for ever, that she would do absolutely anything to secure her goal of immortality.

Animal laughed upon a high rebellious note, singing a tune of happiness she could never have learned by rote.

Vomit dived under the waves. Tiny particles of sand swirled around her.

'Why can't she eat?' Vomit thought. She had hold of Animal's ankles, sticks of bone and sinew. It took a few tugs before Animal tipped over and fell through waves into the underwater world of seaweed and turbulent sand. Animal thrashed about; Vomit dived under her and pushed her body up upon her back as dolphins did for fun. She threw her upon the waves and the waves washed her on to the shore. Animal's chest heaved; her nipples were tight buds. Vomit lay down beside her, Animal greedily sucked in air.

'Can air feed you?' Vomit asked gently, taking Animal's hand while she turned on to her side so she might look at her.

'What feeds you? What feeds your soul?' she asked as she traced the form of Animal's lips. 'Don't you hunger for a future?'

'No,' Animal spoke at last. 'I hunger only for the Great Work. Since I found my Work, I have needed no other sustenance. I have discovered… ' She turned her head away from Vomit's close scrutiny and spat out the gritty bits of salt from her mouth. She wiped her mouth with the back of her hand.

'You can't imagine how changed I am,' Animal continued. 'A transformation from a fake thing, more clothes than creature, posing in artificial programmed mannerisms in response to civilised signals. I see through it all; the layers within me have shifted one upon the other and rubbed each other raw with the agony of self knowledge. Beneath the layers I spied a creature of fabulous beauty, nothing to do with anyone but itself, unclouded by the curse of egoccentricity and convention.' She spat and wiped her mouth again. 'My back is burning in this sun.'

Their eyes met. Vomit saw volcanic fire, red and alive with demonic knowledge gained from first hand experience. 'Oops,' she thought, 'and oops again.'

'Animal, I stink,' she said aloud. 'My hair is matted and I'm sure my facial expression resembles wild boar more than the professional person I once was.'

'Ha!' Animal laughed horribly. She tossed her head back showing black edged teeth and a neck that had more character than the bark of an old oak. A spider crawled upon her white flesh adding to the overall ghoulish effect.

'I shall clean you in great detail,' Animal promised. 'I shall perfume your crevices, massage sweet oils into your thighs, rub berries upon your bleeding feet.'

'Couldn't I just get on with it, make myself respectable and hurry off to Palermo?' asked Vomit.

'Of course! Orders!'

The two naked women ran across the short stretch of beach and then took the path to the water hole where they had abandoned their clothes.

Their shadows were short in high sun. They ran in jerky unpractised movements. They had not run frequently enough to know that energy comes from relaxation and the pit of the stomach.

Panting, as if from more than an hundred metre caper, they clambered up the path, careless of their tender feet. Animal was ahead of Vomit, she stopped and waited for Vomit where she could look out to sea. Her posture was crooked as she stood with hands on uneven hips. She held her head noticeably to the left.

Heroin was diminishing Animal's sense of self although she didn't see it like that. Magick, its drugs and riotous irregular lifestyle, little food and sleep meant that her feet could have been protruding from her navel and she would not have been alarmed. Her mind was weak and hacked away from her upbringing, she believed herself carefree, if sex-deranged. Quite likely her mind was damaged by over stimulation. She couldn't think for herself, didn't think she had to, now she had Great Beast.

Vomit caught her up with her. Sand drifted from their bodies as it dried in the sun. They picked a way along the narrow path, mainly used by goats. Little sticks dug into their ankles. Waves lapped behind them demonstrating a force more tireless than a man's sex drive. Before them they heard water gushing vertically. They gripped each other tightly and grinned, like a pair of sphinxes conveying secret knowledge to those who cared enough to wait for an utterance which came once in each millennium.

Vomit and Animal carried such utterance within their

hearts, the secret of Ipsissimus, Great Beast, 666, just like his mother had said. He knew the philosophic direction of the next generation.

They came to the place where the waterfall plunged into a large pool. Vomit wriggled in where the water was deepest. first her feet and ankles. Then she looked to Animal for encouragement. Vomit slid her whole body in, fantasising that she would spiral down to an underground cavern where lived a sleek water snake and handsome merking.

With head underwater she rubbed the sand out of it. She needed shampoo, soap and a comb; she hadn't done any grooming for a while except to give GB his infernal manicure. She ran her fingers through her hair, pulling out knots as far as she could.

Animal stood in shallow water, laughing ghoulishly, her imagination a place quite apart - sacred/divine/demonic. It was all the same to her, pleasure or pain.

Vomit rubbed water into the marks of time upon her face, rubbing out dirt and dead skin. Animal cackled and splashed as Vomit retrieved her clothes. She held the garments up.

'Can any sense be made of these rags?'

Animal cackled.

'I've lost you, I can see,' continued Vomit. 'You run back to Great Beast. I'll hurry off to Palermo and see what I can find for us all.' And to herself, 'Have to find myself a simple dress to start with.'

She pulled what remained of her tattered frock over her head and shifted it about on her body so that the rips were not so noticeable. She picked up Animal's frock, in better condition than her own. 'I'll never get this on.' Experimentally, she tied it over her shoulders and then tried wearing it wrapped around her hips. At last she decided it looked best worn as a shawl and made a neat, if unconventional, knot with its sleeves at her neck. 'Does this look better?' asked Vomit.

Animal shrugged, her face a picture of a child's huffy mood.

'I'm sorry Animal, I didn't think you'd mind. You'll be alright getting back to the Abbey naked?'

'I have no underwear, dearest. I need to wear something,' Animal sulked.

'If you must have your dress, you must have your dress.' Vomit unknotted the sleeves and handed the dark polka dot piece of material to Animal who gave her a sudden smile, a child's imitation of adult charm, snatched the dress and ran a few metres to pull it on. She smoothed it down over her body with a regal air.

Vomit was as distressed at Animal's deterioration into childlike behaviour as at her own tattily clad condition. She'd beg a garment from a villager - shag Senor Georgio for one if she had to. She'd shagged him for the continuation of their wine supply and she'd shag him for this.

She waved a big gesture goodbye to Animal who seemed quite cheerful, in a lambish kind of way, now she'd got her frock back.

'I'd shag him for free, for fun,' she thought to the bright sun as it poured its lavish rays upon her long damp hair. 'Beats teaching.' There was a spring in her step as she approached the village. 'Find Georgio and avoid his mother and sisters,' she recited as she spied the first black-clad female figure looking gravely at her from the rectangular frame of a doorway.

Vomit was used to the serious stares and the village gossip. The Abbey of *Do What Thou Wilt* spiced up the locals' lives.

'I don't know whether I shall, I don't know whether I shan't.' Vomit sang to herself, thinking of whether she should stay at the Abbey when she returned from her expedition to Palermo. She sang to herself to remain aloof from these grim staring women as she trod the trampled mud between the small stone houses with clean steps.

She felt self-consciously that her bottom wobbled and most likely its cleft could be seen through the inadequate orange and yellow flowered cotton thing she wore. Quite recently it had made an appearance as a worn out tablecloth. She must do something about it.

She and Georgio had a place they met, she made the signal by singing their song softly as she passed his wine shop. General provisions really, though she just thought of it as a wine shop, for that's what she mainly bought, or acquired. He also sold local produce such as fruit, cheese, milk and herbs.

She made her way, via a circuitous route, to a deserted goatherd's hut, a shelter from sudden showers and their usual meeting place. There was a bale of new hay in one corner and an old sheet held fast under a stone. A place to throw off inhibitions for an orgasm or two. Vomit looked at the hay, thought about the arrangements she could be making for their comfort. She didn't want to do anything until he'd actually arrived, didn't want to appear too keen either. If she did she might not get what she wanted, which was more than a frock, a shawl and an orgasm.

She used a stone in a crude attempt to file a nail straight. It was cool in the hut. She had never been a lady of fashion and this rustic style suited her character. Vomit was attractive because she was kind and had a natural empathy for the 'common man'. She was seductive because free of inhibition and moral fibre.

Here came her common man, *homo Latinus vulgaris*. Dark, hairy and so on, quite a living cliché was Senor Georgio.

'Cara mia!'

'My dearest,' she replied.

They embraced, Georgio squashed her big breasts against his hard workman's chest. Her soft bosoms were fine fuel for his growing erection. He squeezed her luscious buttocks and pulled her close against his lingam, so she could feel it against her pudenda. He wanted her to feel how much he wanted to get into her. He kissed her neck and ears with subtlety that belied the crude behaviour of his hips, grinding slowly upon hers. He whispered into her ears, 'How I want you, how lovely you are, how good you smell, how glad I am you have come to me!'

His hands ran up her back into her hair, until he felt her relax upon him. His hands now wanted to be where she was hottest; he reached down for her fine fat yoni, bursting fruitful and juicy ripe.

'Not yet my Georgio.' Vomit broke away. 'You must get me a few things before we continue our connoisseurs' love making.'

'You use me,' he pouted. 'You pretend to love me - it is not true! You come here only when you want things from me! You should come to me for myself, myself alone. And if I give you things, that is alright. I choose that! I! You make demands, you ask for things, our loving is spoiled.'

'Is it?' she asked archly. He opened his mouth. 'No more words,' Vomit commanded. 'Hurry, get me a few things I need, then we can continue!'

He assented.

'I want a dress, a shawl and a lift to Palermo.'

'No! A dress, that is easy. I cannot take you to Palermo.'

'Someone can.'

'Someone! Who is this someone?'

'A donkey. I've got to get there today. I can come back tomorrow on the bus.'

'A donkey, you say, as if a donkey is nothing, as if I can click my fingers and command a donkey.'

'Well you can, can't you?' Vomit insisted.

'Yes, yes, I can I can. First…' he pressed himself against her. She yielded. It would be okay, he would get her to Palermo today.

She fell back on to the hay. He was strong and single minded, unbuckling his belt. Their eyes met in black fire as he pulled down his trousers and his erection burst out and Georgio's iron bar filled the space between them. She had only a moment to wait on the hay before the head of his penis, red and moist with pre-cum parted the lips of her vulva. This moment of entry was a moment of release from tension, nicer for her than the prodding movements he made inside her. There was always the chance of having her cervix bruised or not building up the right level of arousal before he was ready to come inside her.

She concentrated on matching his rhythm. A flash of his faithful wife came before his eyes. Vomit did not feel altogether natural in the rhythm of this shag. He squeezed her buttocks and sucked her nipples, sometimes hard, sometimes gently. His body listened to her, wanting her to bring her whole self into this moment.

He made it easy for her, as she made it easy for him, with her soft white flesh and her supple limbs and sublime cunt muscles dancing within her. Their genitals thus engaged in fucking, were well-matched dance partners. The only witnesses to their skill, their own senses, were slowly obliterated by the process of gradual sensual saturation. They went a long way past the place where decisions are made, on the road to orgasm, the place where everyone is divine, noone has a name and one's journey can not be remembered until all is over.

Georgio turned away from her as his post orgasmic penis shrank. He didn't like to look into the eyes of a woman he had shared love with; he was afraid of what he might find there. Quickly, he pulled up his trousers and kissed her neck. He looked back at her. She was dishevelled and helpless; this satisfied him. He dashed off to arrange transport and get her clothing, pleased to have a job to do so he would not have to dwell on his feelings for her.

Vomit, awry, felt her neck would never again hold her head in the designated position. She felt blasted, her soul routed - as if she'd been tricked into selling for pork, a hoard of piglets she'd been rearing as pets. She was victim of an eternal hunger and that very same unappeasable hunger manifested in a sperm that probed her egg to leave her permanently altered, poised for multiple change on all fronts.

∴ six

6.1 To Palermo

Thus did Vomit set out for Palermo, black clad, in a small donkey cart with three other black clad women. Like them, Vomit had a black shawl wrapped around her head, to hide her hair, shoulders and neck. The shawl was pinned in place with a simple base metal broach that Georgio had brought for her, borrowed from his wife's jewellery case, the simplest he could find in a hurry. In his guilty haste, he forgot that this broach was the first gift he had given his wife, before they were married.

At first the other women eyed Vomit suspiciously, but it

was natural to chatter on a journey and easy for Vomit to join in. She felt good with Georgio's semen oozing out of her yoni. The day smelt good and she liked the smell of herself. She wondered why these women were travelling with her to the city at any hour other than early morning. To be with her, she expected, to extract gossip and to look at her close up, to assess her as a woman. Well, she wouldn't come between them and their feminine assessment, she hoped they could smell the fresh sex on her too.

The women didn't want to know about the strange foreigner's religio-philosophical belief system; they wanted to know if "the Fat One" as they called the Great Beast, was a husband to all the Abbey women and asked her outright.

'Oh no, we are all free people,' Vomit replied casually in Italian. She had many intellectual skills as she had taken her teaching work seriously.

'Free, how do you mean free?' asked the youngest of the women.

'Free to come and go, to do as we please, to be with whoever we want.' Vomit was careful with her accent and emphasis so that this idea sounded lofty, avoiding the implication that the women of Thelema behaved like whores. The three Sicilian women nevertheless did think the women of Thelema were whores, foreign women, their sexuality hanging out of their bodies like sacks of mutilated babies.

'That would not be freedom to me,' said a grandmother. 'Without the mutual trust of fidelity how could we live? How could we bring up our children?'

Vomit was jolted from side to side by the fierce action of wooden wheels upon hard knobbly mud. She thought about other women's husbands: she had never had one of her own, hadn't wanted one, had always wanted a school; well now she was selling her school. Would it be possible for her to teach again - turn the clock back? Could she do that? Could she go through the old motions with effective sincerity? All that ritual shagging and intoning, orgasms and pasta had left marks upon her; she was fatter and more open. Something else too, she was aware of sex. Could she hide that? Did she want to?

Upon reaching Palermo Vomit was thoughtful. She followed Great Beast's instructions carefully and located the café. Fantastic herbal cooking smells made it easy to find. Here she should find the exiled German pharmacist who would get H for her, in the quantity Great Beast required for himself and his womenfolk.

There were only men in the café. Silence reigned as she pushed the door open. She wished she'd been wearing her tatty see-through costume as all those dark male eyes turned upon her; wished she had looked a thousand times less respectable, so those eyes would approach her, ravish her. She wanted to provoke sexual fantasy and erection in every man in the place.

As it was she was dressed in demure black costume. She pushed the shawl from her head to show her hair, in an instinctively brazen gesture. She asked to see Herr W. One man spoke to the manager and a third man was dispatched to fetch the pharmacist. Coffee was put before Vomit and still standing, she sipped it. She surveyed the men, her eyes making sexual invitations.

She asked if there was a ladies' room she could use. 'Not really,' was the reply, 'but Andrio here will show you where you can go.' She followed Andrio into a small white passageway. She was close behind him, almost touching his body, her fast aroused breath upon his neck. He stopped before a door and she pressed herself right up against his buttocks, rotating her loins a little so there would be no doubt in his mind what she wanted.

One hand on the door in front of him, he looked over his shoulder at her and acknowledged the earnestness in her eyes, the eagerness he did not understand but was well prepared to enjoy. His beautiful full standing erection made his trousers tight and uncomfortable. He turned down a cool passageway to the left and led her into a small store room containing sacks of flour and crates of oil. It was dark here except for a little grey light from the white passageway.

He turned around and pushed her against the wall, pressed his lips down upon her, so quickly that their eyes only had time to exchange the most basic message.

In record time, his hands were within her black garment, he reached for her yoni, to feel her wetness. She opened her legs and let out an audible exhalation as his thumb pressed into her wet cunt. Andrio unfastened his trousers. She watched his coarse hands, hairy and square, unequipped for delicate caress, pull the leather of his belt back and release the notch from its metal prong. His hands shook and it was unusually difficult for him to undo his fly buttons.

No speech passed between them, only the sounds of their breath.

She loved to watch as the lingam burst out from trousers. Loved to look at it as long as she could, before it was within her tunnel of delight.

Andrio gave her only a moment to gaze upon his thick penis, two purple veins alive with blood pulsed up its comparatively short length like rivers flowing downhill. 'I am the sea into which his seminal river will pour,' she thought as her muscles dilated to allow his thick rod to penetrate her. He pressed in, in short jabs, which pulled his foreskin back and forth. He had to crouch in some tense awkwardness to get in her properly as they stood, although they were a convenient height in relation to one another for this sexual position. He approached orgasm but she was not so near it and he did nothing to bring her on. Footsteps in the passageway spoke of rescue.

It was Jesu who had come to find where his friend Andrio had got to with the foreign lady. Herr W, the pharmacist, was ready for her.

'Andrio!' Jesu called and smiled on hearing soft groans. He opened the door upon the copulating couple in time to excite Vomit greatly with his voyeuristic services. Today she wanted to be watched while she shagged. Her eyes met

Jesu's. She enjoyed the empathy between the two men. Jesu's penis would be more curved than Andrio's, she intuited, and he would enjoy her orgasm as much as his own, she could see that.

Andrio withdrew. 'Jesu, you bastard,' he said in a comradely manner.

'Now what have we here?' Jesu asked.

'She is all yours,' offered Andrio, wiping his cock with a dirty handkerchief and pulling up his trousers.

'All mine? Straight after you? Not *all* mine.' He kept his eyes on Vomit. 'I will have her nevertheless. I will make her mine for the time it takes to shag. Would you like that?'

'I'll leave you two to it then.' Andrio was not the voyeur that Jesu was.

'We shall shag?' Jesu asked Vomit. She glanced away, made small by his masculinity. He gave himself time to get fully erect before he showed her his lingam. He knew how important it was for the woman to see the lingam as very big, capable of filling her up with pleasure. He decided not to shag her straight away. He'd wait until Andrio's sperm had dribbled out of her, wait until she begged him and then he would take his time with this passionate foreign woman who had come to buy strong drugs.

'Come, let us go to see Herr W.' Vomit's heart dropped. Jesu teased her, would he shag her? She followed him back into the café, where the men were more comfortable with her presence now she had been, as it were, initiated into their company. She had a place among them.

6.2 Good Things

Vomit was quiet and passive as she followed Jesu to where Herr W waited at a table. Her feet made patterns in the sawdust strewn upon the floor as she wound her way between shabby tables. She liked the herbal smell and the dark hairy men with knobbly hands. Jesu's hands were fine, she noted, he was not quite as the others were.

Jesu exchanged a few words with the man who served, the men laughed together a little, but not without a note of respect for her.

Herr W led her through the back entrance of his pharmacy, not open to the public and Jesu followed. She was very aware of him, of wanting to have sexual relations with him. She was pleased to note how he maintained his self-assurance. The more she saw of him, the more she was excited by him. The more her awareness trained itself upon him, the more she saw his uniqueness, his particular attraction, the shape of his earlobes, the slight sneering curl of his upper lip which denoted independence.

Jesu was pleased at her silent attentiveness. He planned an adventure in his mind, what he would do with her. He would make her wait, make her beg. He wanted her eyes to plead with him and her body to be absolutely fluid in expectation of his entrance into her snatch. He wanted her salivating and moaning, trying to concentrate on other tasks but overwhelmed by desire for him.

He teased her with his mind and was glad as a dribble of saliva escaped her lips and her eyes wandered down his body to his crutch where his cock bulged. She discerned the shape of his knob through his trousers, it throbbed and grew stiffer with her eyes' embrace.

Herr W held a flat package.

'You must be very careful with this heroin,' he said to her in German, which she spoke and understood as well as Italian, French, English and Latin. She had taught languages. 'This heroin is very pure, excellent quality; very strong.'

'Isn't this the type Drummond usually has?' asked Vomit taking the package, small for substance other than heroin or diamonds.

'No, absolutely, no. This is far stronger. He will need to use less and it will last him longer. It will also cost him more.'

'Also, I need cocaine.'

'Cocaine, yes,' Herr W looked doubtful. 'You say Herr Drummond is used to this mixture, heroin and cocaine?'

'Oh yes, he has been using them both for many years,' Vomit assured the pharmacist.

'I see, I see.' His sharp little eyes assessed her.

'I shall weigh and wrap the cocaine while you fetch the money, from the Post Office, you said?'

'Yes, thank you, Herr W.'

'That's quite alright, yes, for Herr Drummond quite alright. We play chess,' he added as if this were an excuse for selling him a rather large quantity of a potentially lethal drug combination. People do like to offer an explanation for their natural inclination.

'50 grams of cocaine and 100 grams of heroin, that is correct?'

'Correct,' affirmed Vomit.

They shook hands and Vomit rejoined Jesu who was gracefully loitering outside. He tossed a small stone into the air and caught it skilfully, he'd been doing this for a while and hadn't dropped the stone once.

He wanted to take her to the place he had in mind, where lovemaking could begin. Vomit resisted. 'I must go to the Post Office and collect some money.' Her eyes danced; she had found him out. His eagerness betrayed a hole in his macho control, she would be able to do things to him as well as he to her.

Holding hands, they methodically made their way through the streets to the Post Office where the money, more than twice as much as she'd expected, awaited. After delivering the money to a grateful Herr W, Jesu pulled her into an alley at the first possible opportunity and pressed his lips upon hers. She opened her mouth and their tongues folded one upon the other. Their loins ground together, felt the contours of one another's genitalia. This was going to be more than just another instant game of pleasure. They were both deeply involved in the sexual chemistry of this encounter.

Neither made a move to unbutton and expose flesh. Vomit's hand lay loosely upon Jesu's buttocks, learning his rhythm. She fondled the slope of his hard sex machine muscles. His hand found her waist and the curves that met here. He avoided the areas where nerve cells are closest together, where she was most sensitive.

It was a long kiss. She ran her tongue along the serrated edge of his teeth, licked his gums, wound tongue around tongue. Now their lips alone touched, now the sides of their noses met and breath interwove with breath. Vomit ran her hand through the back of his hair. She was grateful for his response.

They stayed close, quiet, in a long embrace. They enjoyed each other's presence within clothes all the more for expectation of future mutual nakedness.

'Come on, let's go.' He pulled her out of the alley, smoothing his hair. Then took her hand again like a teenage lover. He whistled and she was carefree and happy.

She had wrapped the drug packages together in a black

cloth and put this bundle into her shoulder bag. Great Beast would be so pleased. She was pleased. This pleasure and fulfilment she now knew was a long way from running a school and teaching languages to young ladies. 'I was a young lady once myself,' she thought.

She smiled at Jesu who always knew when to meet her eyes, to reassure her she was doing the right thing, going to the right place, being with him. A relief after Great Beast who was sensitive only to the movement of his own desire, until the woman was dripping fanny juice all over his face and then he would be most attentive to her sexual needs. GB would catch you out, snatch you away from yourself, tie you down with his way of extracting orgasm upon orgasm.

Jesu squeezed her hand, warm and friendly, before releasing it to open a door for her. A door in a row of doors distinguished in no way at all, except it was the door that Jesu and Vomit walked through to the room where they were to finally shag.

∴ seven

7.1 A Wanderer's Return

At *Ridelands* the rain poured down, although it was not to last long. One of Norfolk's charms is that bad weather never lingers for it can be wished away.

It was a warm September; yellow summer light had deepened two shades towards the amber of equinox. It was this amber light that Mama Shag and Est admired through the rain as they stood at the kitchen window.

Mama Shag pointed to the world outside the window and explained something insistently. She wanted Est to accept her version of what had happened to Stritch and where he was now. Est was reluctant to believe Great Beast had nothing to do with Stritch's death and wondered if Mama Shag herself was beholden to GB in some way. Had she finally accepted his authority and spiritual status as Ipsissimus?

Claudia was at school nearby in the village. She had taken her bicycle today and Est wished the rain would ease for her return journey.

The two women moved into the depths of the kitchen where Mama stirred the fennel, leek and ginger soup which simmered on the Aga. They were both interested in flavour, nutrition and the medicinal benefit of herbs. Mama lifted the lid of the heavy pan and savoured the aroma. She turned her head to one side and sneezed violently.

'Bless you,' said Est. She bent down to open the oven door and tapped the top of a coriander and mustard loaf, a savoury surprise designed to eat with the soup. It was a cook together, eat together kind of day.

A wet figure outside spread his hands over two of the small window panes that made up the whole and pressed his nose on the glass. Rain droplets dripped from his hair and his eyelashes and ran down the glass. He could see steaming food and the two women's tangible intimacy. He rested his head sideways upon the glass, making a small thud on impact.

Mama Shag's grey head and Est's honey haired head, turned as one to the form smudged against the window. His body language spoke of the abandonment of normal social intercourse. It was clear that he would make no attempt to present a controlled persona.

Rain fell upon his cheek and soaked into his beard, grown thick upon his chin and cheeks while he'd stalked Est and Claudia. He'd pursued them to Mama Shag's, where he'd watched and waited for a clue to Animal's whereabouts. He didn't want to approach them directly or have to explain himself. He didn't want to lay himself open to any rejection before final union with Animal, however minor and seemingly unimportant it might be, as he suspiciously felt any rejection would imply final rejection at her hands. This union was his obsessive goal.

Est had accomplished her obsessive goal, had run her quarry to ground by finding her Magician first in Stritch and then in GB. Her dreams had manifested and she had nothing left to do but live. Meantime, Mahoney had inherited the primal energy of the hunt.

The rain eased. His clothes were sodden right through to his vest. Even his skin was damp. At last, Mahoney unconditionally opened himself. Never brave, it wasn't until the nadir of fatigue that he realised he had to approach Est. He needed help; all his dreams were connected to Animal, the true Animal, goddess and whore. His life could not be properly lived until he had unravelled the myth that she was. She was the source of his poetry and through devotion to her he would find the full flow of artistic continuum, the same artistic continuity and spiritual inspiration that Est had discovered through the Magician.

Est came to the window, saw the desperate face. She was unfazed by this apparition: 'I know him!' she called to Mama Shag, who was ladling out three bowls of aromatic soup. 'He's been following us since we arrived back in Paris. I think he's something to do with Great Beast.'

'Yes?' Mama Shag placed the savoury loaf on a cooling rack. She laid the table with plates, napkins and a long bread knife.

'I'll bring him in.'

'Do that.' Mama Shag served up soup and put the pan back on the Aga. She licked her fennel flavoured fingers and tore off a serrated nail with her teeth.

Est brought in zombie Mahoney. He was shivering and so she wrapped him in a coarse wool blanket hemmed roughly with red blanket stitch.

'I know him too. He was here with Animal,' Mama declared.

'When I was here?' asked Est.

'I'm not sure,' Mama hedged her bets.

Mama Shag helped seat Mahoney. Silently, they fed him a little warm soup before undressing him. Dirty water from his clothes made a puddle around the legs of the chair. The kitchen warmth revived him although he hadn't got dangerously cold as it was a warm early autumn.

He tried to eat, but no soup remained in the spoon by the

time it reached his mouth. Robotically, he repeated this ineffectual eating procedure, looking all set to play this part ad infinitum, splattering the broth down his soiled coat.

The two women laughed over their soup. Mama Shag took pity on him and fed him, giving directions as one would to a toddler.

'Open your mouth. Good, in it goes. Close your mouth. That's right, tilt your head back, swallow. *No*, swallow. Try it yourself. Never mind here's another spoonful.'

When he had eaten a little, Est attended to his clothes. 'Lift up your arm. Get this wet coat off, it weighs a ton. How many layers of clothing have you got on?' And to Mama, 'Claudia will be back soon. I'd like to get him to bed before she's home.'

'Yes, I agree. He's managing the soup. I don't think there's anything wrong with him. Exhaustion mainly.'

'And hunger,' added Est.

'Starvation.' Although Mahoney was a big fellow, his cheeks were sunken.

'I doubt if he's eaten much while he's been following us,' Est offered, identifying him as their Paris stalker.

'I shouldn't think so. I'm not going to be able to get him to eat bread.'

Mama Shag's creased face wrinkled into a big smile as Est struggled with Mahoney's trouser fly.

'What are you looking for down there?' she cracked. 'A solution to all your artistic dilemmas?'

'Protection against your holier-than-thou regime.' Est managed the first button but was in for a shock. 'Ugh.'

'Urine?'

'I should say so. Fresh and wet! I can survive this; I only hope there isn't more to come.'

'I expect there is. Probably hasn't pulled his trousers down for a week.'

'And ejaculated into them too by the look of it.' Est soldiered on bravely with her repulsive task.

'Don't you mean, the feel of things, rather than the look?' Mama Shag cut and chewed on a slice of the fresh loaf, not put off her food by watching the unwrapping of Mahoney and the revelation of copious slime within the mummy-like layers of his clothing.

'I'll get an old sack to put his vile clothes in,' offered Mama.

She sang a lullaby as she went to the hardware cupboard to the left of the sink to get a hessian potato sack. She never threw useful articles away but stored them up until they came in handy.

'And a pair of scissors,' Est called, 'to cut these trousers from under his bottom. I think he's gone to sleep.'

'With his head in the soup?' Mama Shag collected up coat, shirt, vest and socks; then rolled them into neat parcels so all the items would fit into the sack. She let the surplus water slosh on to the flagstone floor.

'Ask him to stand up. I don't think he's as unconscious as he appears.'

'You ask him,' huffed Est. It was a nasty job.

'Stand up love, there's a dear,' soothed Mama Shag, tipping him under the chin. Obediently Mahoney stood, though made no other sign of life. Est jerked the trousers and underpants down his hairy legs.

'What a fine boy you are!' Mama Shag exclaimed as Mahoney's curled slug was revealed, very much at peace and sleeping. Est gave her a cross look as she lifted his white feet, skin puckered washerwoman style, through his trousers.

'Naked at last.' Mama admired his loose white skin, stained with smudged bits of nature picked up in his wanderings.

'Claudia will walk through the door at any moment,' grumbled Est.

Mama Shag shrugged. 'Help me get this creature up to bed.'

'And dirty our sheets?' Est felt fussy with bad temper.

'Well, do you want to get this hulking great hunk in and out of the tub?' Mama Shag's eyes danced.

'Well, no.'

'Then, to bed!'

Mahoney meekly complied as they guided him through the dining room, down three turns of narrow corridor that joined the utility area of the house with the main rooms. They led him up the stairs, on to the landing, where he stood bare bottomed as the main door burst open.

Claudia had brought a friend home, Polly, and wanted to show her the house. The two girls, in their tidy bottle green uniforms and sensible brown lace up shoes erupted into a fit of giggles at the sight of Mahoney's white moon cheeks. They rushed through the hall way, their heavy shoes thumping the floorboards through the thin carpet. They dashed into the Music Room. Claudia went straight over to the piano, opened the lid and started bashing away at it, unmusically. The bashing turned to tinkles and slowly a tune emerged, a version of *Chopsticks*. Polly flung her satchel into a chintz sofa and, arms aspread spun around in time to Claudia's rudimentary music.

Upstairs, Mahoney's bare feet shuffled along the linoleum. They were going to put him in the room in the West Wing he'd shared with Animal, when he had last stayed at *Ridelands*. They didn't want him in their private quarters.

'Are you sure he'll be alright here on his own?' fussed Est.

'We're not far away and if he moves we'll hear him. He's a noisy one.'

'I suppose so.'

'He only needs warmth and rest,' Mama Shag reassured, stroking Est's hair in a series of long slow gestures as the two woman stood by the iron bedstead where Mahoney lay with his eyes half open, his breathing shallow and irregular.

'Shouldn't we call the doctor?' worried Est. Anxiety dug three grooves in her forehead.

'What could he do?'

'But he isn't sleeping. The doctor would take the responsibility away from us.'

'Are you frightened he's going to die?' Mama Shag's eyes laughed at the younger woman.

'Not die, but never go to sleep or never wake up.'

'A coma?' prompted Mama Shag.

'Perhaps.' Est turned the idea slowly over in her mind. 'He doesn't seem very relaxed.'

Mama leant over and stroked Mahoney's cheeks, then she pinched his ear lobe. The man sighed deeply opened his eyes, closed them, sighed again and settled into slow steady breathing.

'You sleep now.' Mama Shag felt the temperature of his hands and satisfied they were warm, tucked them under the sheets.

'It isn't very cold,' she said to Est. 'It's only September. The bricks still hold the heat of the summer and we haven't had enough rain to make it too humid.'

She stepped back from the bed and folded her hands one over another neatly as she stood beside Est, watching Mahoney as he lay on his back, still as a sleeping knight. Rainwater from his shock of red curls was gradually absorbed by the thick white towel they had spread beneath his head. His chest expanded and the bed clothes rose, he exhaled and they fell.

'He'll be fine,' asserted Mama Shag. 'Let's leave him.' She put a hand on Est's arm.

Est leant forward to put her hand upon Mahoney's forehead. He flinched and began to sit up. Est jumped back, while, with a strong arm, Mama Shag pushed him back down into the soft pillows.

'There now,' she soothed, 'go back to sleep.' In obedient relief he relaxed.

'Why did he do that?' whispered Est.

Mama Shag put a finger to her lips, 'Hush' and indicated the door with her head. 'Come on.'

*   *   *

'Hello Claudia, Hello Polly.' Est greeted the girls cheerfully; they were leafing through back numbers of fashion magazines huddled up on the Music Room sofa. 'Did you have a good day at school?'

'It was alright.' Claudia did not look up from a picture of a green wool suit with red hat, shoes and handbag.

'And how was my day, aren't you going to ask? And what is that strange man doing in the house?'

'How was your day and who was that strange *naked* man?' Claudia's eyes met Polly's, they giggled.

'Two months ago, seems like three years.' This from Est,

a comment on how much Claudia had changed, matured since having a life of her own, friends too, at school.

'We're starving,' Claudia declared.

'I'll bring you tea in here if you'd like? What was the piece you were playing on the piano, so full of feeling and expression?'

'Don't go on, Est. Please.' Claudia was embarrassed.

'Okay. And that man is an old friend of Animal's. He'll be staying I should think, for a few weeks.'

'Or months,' added Mama Shag. 'He may never go.' This last delivered enigmatically as she stood before the bay window, thinking that the grass needed cutting or nibbling by sheep. Peacefully her eyes alighted on the fountain, ha-ha and beyond to the park. The wide emptiness before her was her own domain, an uninterrupted space of trees and animals where she could develop her thoughts unhindered. She imagined herself walking across the park, beneath trees, with dew upon the grass. Birds made domestic noises in the trees; they were half tame through plenty.

'There is abundance at *Ridelands* for humans too,' Mama thought, but her heart was cold. The core of her heart was closed tight as an unripe walnut. All dreams and wishes that could have propelled her into a world of love were frozen and enclosed by time, season and temperature. Powerful forces separated her from spontaneous emotion; she was equally alienated from joy as from despair.

It had been this way since her husband had died. She had

turned from the coldness in her heart to ideas, activities. Turned away from animal warmth and directed her mind to enquiries about the soul. Perhaps there she would rediscover her beloved husband and her self-esteem, hidden within all the emotions that had withered and stagnated upon his death. She felt like a dying tree, roots reaching into quicksand for nutrition where all they found was foul water and sand and a sucking sensation as her trunk slowly sank. The exploration of her roots downwards, searching for life blood, only served to assist the vacuous momentum down, into the fetid pit of quicksand.

'I'll make tea,' she said, wanting to be busy. 'Est, you stay with the girls.' An order, more or less. Est shrugged. What did it matter who made tea, although she took pleasure in these domestic routines, new to her artist's life. To have breakfast, lunch, tea and dinner, supper too; all this was novel and for the moment, a delight, until a new wave of inspiration struck her being and shook her very particles, impelling her to restructure and reassemble all energy for one purpose; creative interpretation upon canvas. Whereupon she would attempt to mutate her very DNA if that would make her a better painter.

For the time being the civilised delights of many meals and taking care of one's appearance satisfied her. Clean nails, brushed hair, white gleaming teeth, sweet breath, polished shoes; this was the stuff of leisure.

7.2 Tea in the Music Room

Est loafed in a chintz armchair. She thought about the Lady of the House, her friend and mentor. Mama Shag's company was a mixed bag of physical energy, spiritual ennui, contrary emotions combined with a party sensibility. She would use the tactics of fun in all situations.

'Too restricting,' Est murmured, 'too taut, too obedient to an invisible set of rules that are quite impossible to decipher.' She mulled over Mama Shag's character. It was a luxury to ruminate so, now Claudia's schooling meant she had time spare after the business of mothering and painting.

She felt liberated, glad that her painting would be enriched by more homely and human details than usually identified her canvas.

'Mama as a great polar bear, the pure consciousness of planet earth, metaphorically materialised, could make a very good subject for a painting.' Est's mind ran on to the practical matter of whether she wanted to establish a studio in this great house. Did she want to make that type of commitment in an environment that was essentially Mama Shag's dominion? She had already committed to stay in the area, to give Claudia's schooling continuity. 'This house?' she hummed. 'This house.'

Mama Shag put her head round the door. 'Tea,' she called.

While Mama Shag brought tea in, Est sauntered across the corridor to the room opposite where many glass cases were piled up containing various dead stuffed birds, butterflies and small mammals. 'God knows why they're here,' Est thought. The sheen on a pheasant's tail had been indefinitely preserved by the taxidermist's art.

Est felt floaty and feminine, a thousand elements of philosophy and psychology rose up and exploded into ideas. She was infused with the heady exhilaration of inspiration. 'I shall have to set up work space.'

Back in the Music Room she gracefully arranged herself in a tatty chair of appealing art deco shape. Mama came in with tea; they were joined by Claudia and Polly. Est folded her legs to one side and crossed her ankles, accepted tea with an understated, 'Thank you.' She took refuge in the tea ritual.

Claudia helped herself to a chocolate éclair from the tea trolley, the upper layer of which carried the teapot, cups, milk, and three types of sugar: demerara, sparkling white lump, and dark sticky muscavado that would turn even the lightest Darjeeling a deceptive treacle brown.

On the lower layer of the trolley, out of immediate view, were the cakes the girls liked so much when they came in from school. Only Est did not have a cake. The other three females, Mama Shag, Claudia and Polly all had cake served on small bone china tea plates with pink roses around the edge. There were chocolate éclairs, coffee éclairs and two small cream horns.

The chocolate éclairs were long and very large, almost too fat to bite on. Once in the mouth they melted; the charm of choux pastry is its insubstantiality in contrast to the fat ooze of whipped cream. Then there was the fondant topping, dark chocolate softened with a little butter and sweetened with icing sugar. Tantalisingly it did not quite reach to the edges of the cake but lay on the top as an island of chocolate in a sea of choux.

Claudia looked at Polly and Polly looked at Claudia. In conspiracy of indulgence they each separated a long éclair from its delicately pleated wrapper, a thread of gold patterning the translucent paper folds. The cake left a fat stain behind it and a few brown splashes where chocolate fondant had touched paper.

Polly was the tiniest fraction of reaction behind Claudia as they opened their mouths wide to eat, not wanting to get chocolate on their lips. The éclairs were consumed with a shoving action. Polly and Claudia didn't care that they got crumbs on their school uniforms and had to open their mouths very wide.

The coffee coated éclairs were much smaller, more like bullets than bombs. Mama Shag took three.

Embarrassment lay between the girls as they finished their cakes and gulped tea. What now? What could follow such a display? They couldn't continue with cream horns; it would be too much.

The sun was on their side of the room and reminded them of another world, quite apart from tea and femininity.

'May we go and play, Est?'

Est nodded. The girls got up quickly; crumbs fell on to the Chinese carpet.

'Don't get your uniforms dirty. Wouldn't you like to change before you go out? Is Polly staying the night?' asked Est, surprised to find how anxious her voice sounded. 'I must paint,' she reminded herself.

'We won't be out long!' called Claudia. 'We'll change later. Don't worry. Polly's mother says she can stay the night as long as she's in good time for school tomorrow.'

They left through the glazed door to the grounds, with the Music and Taxidermy Rooms either side, before Est had time to comment.

'What was that, dear?' asked Mama Shag, looking up from a small pamphlet entitled *Shrinkers and Justice, Man and Nature - Law as it should be and how it is*. A coffee éclair sat on her plate, ignored but not forgotten.

'I want to set up studio,' Est paused theatrically. 'Can I use the room there?' She indicated the Taxidermy Room.

'Why of course. Wouldn't you rather a more private place, upstairs perhaps?'

'I like to see comings and goings, to be part of the world, not to be too self-absorbed.'

'I'll be glad for you to paint.' Mama Shag picked up her coffee éclair.

'You'd only be disturbed upstairs by that man continually pacing up and down moaning, "Animal! Animal!" ' Mama Shag imitated Mahoney, Hound No. 5.

'It would only make him worse if he met up with her.' Est referred to the woman he was obsessed with, Animal.

'You think so?' Mama Shag poured them both more tea, kept warm by a hand knitted cosy.

'I do. She is not the person she was,' Est said.

'If she ever was human, I never noticed.'

'Don't, Mama. She won't move away from Great Beast. She won't even eat unless he says "Animal, eat!" and then only a morsel. She doesn't wash, she stinks!'

Mama nibbled her éclair. 'In a way I'm glad we never got close. It is so worrying to see her like that. Is there anyone else there?'

'Vomit.' Est paused as she took a sip of tea. 'But although she's more sensible, she hasn't got time for anything but shagging.'

'Maybe it would be good if our friend the Hound of the

Baskervilles went to Cefalù and looked after Animal?'
Mama suppressed a cackle.

'He doesn't see her as a real person, someone who has
bodily needs. I can't imagine he'd be aware of the mental
pressures she's under now. She was vulnerable enough in
that department in the first place. No, our beloved groaning
night-howling Hound No. 5 thinks of her as an extension
of his own ego, that part of himself he currently finds and
loses, loses and finds in the rhythm of a long, long wank.
His mission is to shag her every which way.' Est tucked her
feet under her thighs.

'Every *which* way? You must tell me about that
sometime,' Mama suggested.

'You have nothing to learn from their sexual behaviour,
I can assure you. But I expect he considers it mighty daring,
athletic and so on.'

'I think we should send him off to the Abbey and see
what happens. Great Beast will sort him out, or give him
something to think about.'

'I'm not sure Great Beast is staying there.'

'Oh?' Mama queried.

'Well, money is very up and down. His drug addiction is
a big problem for him. He needs a steady supply or his
whole constitution begins to break up. He was talking about
writing a book, about his life, to make money.'

'An autobiography?' queried Mama.

The two women gazed at the girls playing around on the
lawn.

'Yes, except he calls it an auto*hagi*ography. He always has to be different. He's thinking of continuing to write it somewhere he can get drugs regularly.'

'Paris?'

'Not Paris, I think, he has left too many debts behind him there. Maybe London. He may want to write here.' Est raised her eyebrows over her teacup.

'We'll see.' Mama Shag was quite undisturbed at this idea and returned to her sober pamphlet.

'I'll take some tea to our resident ghost.'

'Soothe his spirit - take him those cream horns.' Mama indicated the crumbly pastries generously dusted with icing sugar.

'The power of the cream horn to soothe the half-mad soul. I feel a pamphlet coming on.'

Est wheeled the tea trolley out of the Music Room. She could hear the girls' voices as they played on the lawn and around the fountain, saw the blurred outline of their green clad figures as they ran hither and thither.

She pushed the tea trolley down the corridor. Her mind retained images of the girlish figures. Ideas for paintings jostled with one another, joining together then separating and regrouping as she organised Hound No. 5's tea tray.

7.3 Letter From Cefalù

'I don't think we need worry about anything,' Mama Shag asserted.

'No?' Est put down her thickly buttered toast and took a big swig of coffee.

'No, nothing at all. Well, that's not true. I'm being heartless. I should say nothing to worry about so far as Hound No. 5's concerned.' Mama Shag continued to chew on the gritty millet flakes she added to her porridge. Intermittently she picked her grey teeth with a tooth pick, while she read from a battered piece of paper that had arrived that very morning with the post. The usual mass of administration for the key local figure, Mama Shag.

'He still hasn't said an intelligible word.'

It had been five weeks since Hound No. 5 had returned. Cool golden light came in through the high kitchen window, illuminating the empty place with chair askew and a half chewed crust upon the plate, the place Claudia had hurriedly vacated as she'd left for school. 'Is all he has done for more than a month,' continued Est, 'is groan, "Animal" and take to his bed. Do you remember what happened when I suggested to him that he should participate in the household management?'

'Really?' Mama Shag's mind was on the letter.

'What does the letter say then?'

Mama Shag turned the letter over slowly to read the few lines written on the reverse. One corner of it had been torn off. Mama Shag smoothed the letter out upon the tablecloth with a firm stroking movement and it tore in two.

'Do you want the good news first, or the bad?'

'Which is the most extreme?' Est's brow furrowed as she caught Mama's mood.

'The bad news is as bad as possible, the good I have my reservations about.'

'Bad for me personally, for Thelemites generally or for Great Beast in particular?' asked Est who could not resist turning the contents of the letter into something of a game. Her painting was going well, the studio was her best ever and the canvases were selling like hot cakes. Claudia was enjoying school and actually learning, while dear kind Maltby showed signs of recovery. She'd heard from the sanatorium last week; in the New Year she and Claudia could visit and probably bring Maltby back to *Ridelands*.

As she waited in the morning silence for Mama Shag to read the letter, she searched for a suitable adjective to describe this house. Lovely it certainly was, even with a semi-lunatic poet groaning in an upstairs chamber and the Lady of the House inclined to forays to a shack in her wood where she'd dance naked round a bonfire. Est suspected she herself was guilty of unpardonable eccentricity, for instance, making money. She laughed to herself; *Ridelands* was an interesting, even iconoclastic place to be.

'This letter is from Vomit,' stated Mama.

'The school teacher?'

'Mm, it seems she's pregnant and has left the Abbey, has returned to America. Her sister came and collected her, insisted on her return.'

'Saved her the decision.' Est did not feel involved with the letter. The success of her art had taken her away from her past, away from vulnerability to a safe place. With the drifting and the vulnerability, a lot of the compulsively nervous inclination of her character had gone too. Stritch appeared to her less often and when he did, the hauntings were less real.

Great Beast didn't seem real to her now either. She wondered how she could ever have been obsessed with either of them, though she knew she had been. If her mind could be bothered to come to any conclusion about this, it had to be a cliché about initially believing that what one was looking for was outside the self whereas as the quest progressed one discovered one's journey was essentially inward.

'Is the baby Great Beast's?'

'Yes,' pondered Mama Shag. 'She says the Great Ritual of Magickal Impregnation was successful and both she and Animal are big with the child of Ra-Hoor-Khuit who came to them via the Ipsissimus, the Great Beast.' Mama turned the torn top half of the letter over. 'There's a post script from Animal.' She passed the letter across the kitchen table to Est and pointed to where the hand changed from a fairly confident adult script in ink, to a postscript in childlike pencil. The letters were of irregular size, some words ran into one another.

'It seems that Vomit wrote this letter,' continued Mama Shag, swilling milky tea through her teeth, 'before she left with her sister, but did not post it. She must have left it lying around at the Abbey and when Animal needed to write to us, this was all the paper she could find. She had no money to cable, so she added this postscript at the bottom. "Pet dead. I follow Great Beast to Paris and on to you. Great Beast says, "When the trees are bare and the women are ready to share, they need the charismatic flair of the Ipsissimus. Love, Animal." '

Est spluttered. Her eyes met Mama Shag's and they tacitly agreed not to mull over Pet's alleged death. They wanted to hold on to the easy and satisfying companionship that had been theirs these autumnal weeks.

Est stretched her fingers in the golden light. She wore trousers spattered with white primer. Although she painted neatly with colours, she tended to get messy while preparing the canvas surface. Often relationships too would get tricky when she began a major batch of canvases.

Currently, she was coming to the end of a creative cycle and wanted to paint steadily for a few more months before resting, did not want to be interrupted by Beastly demands for cunt and drug money, for whores and occult highs.

'I don't want to know about Beast and what happens around him.' Est clearly imagined the heavy faced fellow with immobile eyes possessed of a stronger power of penetration than most men's penises. 'He's not a man, is he?' Est paced up and down now, trying to shake off oppressive feelings. There was only one he she could be referring to and that was the GB.

'Not a man? I rather think he is.' Mama Shag leant back, her chair creaked. She laid her hands across her stomach in a complacent gesture.

'Don't let him hear you say that.' Est was generally in awe of GB.

'He wouldn't hear that even if I shouted it in his ear.' Mama was cavalier.

'Not if you tattooed it across some nubile arse?' Est suggested.

'He'd turn the lights on and get on with the buggery.'

'Across his tombstone I shall write,' Est pulled on her canvas shoes, tied the laces, 'here lies Drummond, he turned on the light and entered the dark.'

'Are you going to paint?' asked Mama Shag, wanting to delay Est to talk the letter through.

'There is nothing else I can do; I've no control over him. I assume this means that Animal is pregnant and coming here for nativity? She'll be rolling mad, you know.'

'Mmm.' Mama Shag stared at Est. Est avoided her eye; she was going to paint.

7.4 Rumbles of Great Beast

Ridelands was like a doll's house with each doll in the appropriate room busily fulfilling its function. Est was in her studio; she'd rolled the carpet to one side of the room so it didn't get ruined by paint. High shelves were cluttered with the controversial art of the taxidermist. Small wooden school chairs were pushed to the edge of the room, their seats polished by years of use.

Supreme doll of the house, Our Lady, mother figure, capable of dishing out more than anxiety and breast milk, was in the kitchen preparing a tray. She took an egg from a pan of simmering water on the Aga and peeled it in a bowl of cold water. She then laid it out with toast, nuts and raisins and garnished the food with marjoram and parsley from the kitchen garden.

The tray was for Hound No. 5 who was not known for his expertise with superfluous crockery (like an egg cup) or cutlery of any description. He could more or less deal with the concept of a tray with a plate and a cup upon it as the containers of food and drink. The wild man in him had been aroused by magick and was proving tenacious. His primitive obsession with Animal was alive and uncomfortably virile.

'Maybe he's in love,' allowed Mama Shag as she kicked open the kitchen door and climbed up the oak staircase to the room in the doll's house where Hound No. 5 groaned.

This room was part of a self-contained flatlet, in the West Wing, often assigned to guests on first contact with the Order. Cooking and washing facilities were ensuite, thus some independence could be maintained, for both the newcomer and the Order.

He had not left the apartment for five weeks. He had been calling for thick curtains, for though he kept the blinds drawn they were slatted and let in too much light and view of the outside world for his liking. No thick curtains had been produced. Mama Shag brought him two trays a day, generally around 10 a.m. and 4 p.m. taking away the old tray as she brought the new. Apart from that, she left him to his ranting and masturbating.

Mama sniffed, Hound's rank odour was intense. The letter had come in time. She was pretty sure that for all his inconsolable insomnia and bad hygiene he had not irreversibly progressed in the wild man stakes.

She put the tray down and casually remarked, 'We've had news from Cefalù; Animal is on her way here.' She hesitated, he fell out of bed and got in a muddle with a sheet twisted around him. He thrashed about to free himself. Gratefully Mama Shag noted that he wore the pyjama bottoms she'd left out for him. He freed himself and made his way to her on all fours with his tongue lolling out. He lifted his hands, as a dog would lift his front paws to beg.

Mama Shag humoured his dog behaviour and chucked him under the chin. She saw in his eyes that he had heard the news about Animal.

'You look a mess.' She hoped this small comment would prompt him to tidy to himself up for Animal. 'I shan't bring a tray this afternoon, you can eat with us, 5.30 p.m, tea time. Try to look respectable. Claudia's bringing a friend home from school.'

The thrill that her news sent through Hound No. 5 was quite equal to the thrill Mama felt as the phantom of cloaked Ipsissimus appeared before her, instructing her to make the house ready for his presence. She banished all extraneous thought from her mind, a process which brought her new power.

GB would bring chaos into the house; it was always a time of tremendous renewal at *Ridelands* when Mama's orderly domestic systems were blasted by Great Beast. Then he left; he never stayed long. He couldn't stand the cleanliness nor her righteous holier than thouness for long. She was a force of order to match his own of chaos.

In contrast, Est did not feel good about the prospect of

either Ipsissimus's or Animal's arrival. She wanted to carry on painting undisturbed. And she didn't want Claudia's life made strange. 'I don't want to even tell her they're coming here; I don't want them to come here,' she repeated in a mantra as she applied sky blue paint to a skyscape. 'Why shouldn't my painting come first? Why does magick have to come before art? Why can't he rush around stretching my canvases and sharpening my pencils? Why does everyone have to be in his power? Why can't he be in my power?'

She didn't really believe in Pet's death; kept her mind away from that, away from Stritch's death too. She squeezed herself into pictures of sky, didn't want to see/feel/hear ghosts, didn't want to make love, wanted to paint, wanted Claudia to have the chance of an education.

∴ eight

8.1 Coming Together

Hound No. 5's bare feet slapped on the stairs as he descended one step at a time. He groaned at every movement. 'You don't know what it's like!' His pyjama top flapped on a white belly with loose skin around the navel. Slap! He managed one more step. 'You don't know how I feel.' He leant against the banister. His matted hair stuck out in half formed dreadlocks. He groaned theatrically and hoisted up his blue and white striped pyjama bottoms. He fiddled with the frayed ends of the limp cord that held them up.

His tummy rumbled; he threw his head back and veritably roared. 'Feed me!' The motive that prompted him to emerge from the West Wing apartment for the first time in six weeks was hunger.

Claudia and Polly, coming in from school, caught him having one of his moments again, this time roaring. They giggled and, hungry themselves, clattered to the kitchen, bumping (hips and heads) into one another.

Hound No. 5 took another step. He complained about splinters in his feet and eyes that watched him. Did he mean the stuffed owls? Or was he recalling another night time when he had stood on this same staircase on his way to becoming more than a misplaced poet?

'Feed me!' He bumped on to his bottom and slid down the remaining steps, gathering momentum as he went. 'Oo...er...' he complained at each bump, until he got to the bottom, a semi-coordinated mess.

An irregular lifestyle and a fatalistic attitude towards feeding himself, or being fed, as he looked at it, had done nothing for his physical condition. He had left it to the powers that be to provide for him. The initial idea had come from a superficial survey of Buddha's life. He'd lived in a wood hadn't he, during his search for the end of all mankind's suffering? And he'd sat under a tree, hadn't he? With a bowl held between patrician hands, he'd eaten only what fell from the sky into his bowl, a scanty fare of berries and nuts.

Hound No. 5's idea was fundamentally skewed asceticism. It is one thing to sit under the Tree of Enlightenment and perfect a religion of openness and devotion. It is another to wander upon the globe with a huge gaping mouth, jaws ready to chomp on anything that might be thrust into the red chasm, with a self-dramatising *feed me* attitude. It was remarkable that this series of behaviours had, through sheer passion, developed into a genuine quest.

Poor Hound No. 5 loved his grub. He salivated as tasty food aromas wafted through *Ridelands*. He peeped around the kitchen door holding his pyjama bottoms up with one hand. His every pore cried, 'feed me.' But it wasn't only actual food he called out for, nor sex, nor for the meaning of life. It was for the experience of being fed, of feeling sex, awareness of life; for passion, intensity and poetry. His charm was this intensity that he could plug into at Will.

His heart throbbed with the mantra which animated his squashy tomato lips. 'Animal, Animal, my Animal.' His breath smelt like catshit, his hair was a breeding place for lice; bed bug bites beaded his ankles; yet passion made him big, red and beautiful. He trembled before the company assembled round the kitchen table.

Claudia and Polly giggled and scraped their chair legs on the stone flags. Then Ipsissimus rose from his place at table to greet his Hound of Darkness, amiably.

'Hound, how good of you to join us. Our generous

hostess told us to expect you. Sit down fellow, sit down.' He indicated the vacant seat at the end of the table, where Mahoney the Hound's back would be directed towards the kitchen sink.

Ipsissimus had brought Animal with him from Cefalù. Ipsissimus sat to the right of Hound with Animal on his right and Est opposite. The girls and Mama Shag sat in a separate cluster at the far end of the table. Est glanced anxiously towards her daughter. So far so alright. Claudia didn't seem much interested in the new arrivals. She kept away from them in a healthy easygoing kind of way; she showed no sign of fascination with these exotic nocturnal beings.

'May I help to you to partridge?' Est offered Ipsissimus a steaming plate of small game coated in sticky gravy.

'Succulent partridge with chestnut, honey and cinnamon, no doubt?'

Est nodded, adding, 'Cooked with a little Alsace.'

'Mmm.' He sniffed the food extravagantly. 'You spoil me.'

Est's eyes met Ipsissimus's, 'Damn it,' she thought, 'Claudia might not be fascinated, but I am.' She looked at him sideways. 'Sex stirs,' she noted of herself. She also noted she was sending indulgent feminine smiles his way and had a decided inclination to ripple her spine in his direction. 'Damn.' She bit her lip as Ipsissimus's eyes lingered a moment on her lips with infuriating power in his diamond eyes.

Vegetables were passed around the table. Claudia and Polly picked at their food. They were mostly enwrapped in conspiratorial simperings, including Mama Shag in a small way, a token adult protector of their private pubescent world.

Hound No. 5 faced his loved one and did not know what to say. He wanted to take her upstairs and be alone with her in the West Wing apartment but he was not even able to catch her eye. He took a great gulp of the rich burgundy that Est passed him; too big a gulp, he choked and just managed to turn his head to one side so the burgundy would spurt on to the floor rather than somewhere less socially acceptable.

Animal was inanimate, her hands folded in her lap, arms bare as usual in a short sleeved frock. She stared at her lap, she could have been asleep 'cept she twitched when a fly landed on her cheek. She was very thin. Blue veins wriggled their way to her extremities through taut skin, like fuses ready to be lit.

Ipsissimus's attention was for Est alone. The rest of the party receded into the background, the girls' chatter, Hound No. 5's slobbering, Animal's doom laden presence, Mama Shag's hostess attentiveness. Est was hyper-aware of Ipsissimus, of his lips groping for food, his flabby cheeks wobbling as he chewed, but most of all his eyes; they drilled into her even as he fed himself.

Est couldn't really eat; her stomach was tight with nervous energy. She fiddled with the thick sticky gravy, licked the ends of the fork and pushed the flavour around her mouth. She didn't really like game; the smell of it made her feel sick.

'Est, can we leave the table?' asked Claudia quietly. She didn't want to attract *his* attention.

'Sorry?' Est was a long way off.

'Can we...?' began Claudia.

'Of course, yes of course, sorry. Does your mother know you're staying tonight, Polly?'

Claudia gave her an angry *of course she does* look. Est nodded permission.

Released from the growing tension between Est and Ipsissimus, the girls made as much noise as possible screeching their chair legs as they left the table. Est frowned but said nothing as they rushed outside into evening's orange haze. They scattered footprints across the dew laden grass, jumped down the ha-ha and ran into the wood where life rustled within fallen leaves and shafts of sun made carnival patterns through trees.

Hound No. 5 helped himself generously to partridge. Est and Mama Shag had prepared six birds. Ipsissimus and Hound No. 5 more or less ate three a piece. They gorged themselves. Ipsissimus ate tidily and muttered appreciative comments about the tenderness of the breast, the subtlety of the sauce. He guessed the various herbs and spices used. Hound No. 5 ate carnivorously, dripping food on to the . table. He abandoned cutlery and used fingers, found fingers too fussy so raised the plate to mouth and poured gravy down his gullet.

Mama Shag cleared the girls' plates away.

'They can have dessert when they come in,' she said to no one in particular. She moved slowly, for once, tired. 'Can you do the washing-up, Est? I must go and sit down.'

'I'll get the girls to do it,' Est organised automatically, preoccupied with Ipsissimus.

Sleepily, Mama Shag shuffled through a humble doorway resembling the entrance to a broom cupboard. It led up a steep twist of woodwormy steps to a latched door. Click, finger down on the latch. The door stuck then opened. Mama Shag paused, breathless. She was sleepy but pleased to return to her cosy East Wing apartment, overlooking the kitchen garden. She had lived in these old housekeeper's rooms, since her good husband had died.

Hound No. 5 ate the last potato by jamming it uncut into his ravenous mouth. He couldn't remember the last time he'd eaten. Neither could he recall when Animal had last been in his arms.

'Animal, Animal, my Animal,' he groaned and slipped off his chair with a bump that prostrated him. He rolled over on to his belly. His limbs contorted in ineffective swimming gestures. Clumsily he got on to all fours and crawled behind Ipsissimus to lift his head on to Animal's lap. She twirled a coil of his hair around a finger then pushed him away. He crawled under the table where he curled up around her red slippered feet. He began to snore, gustily.

The blind was already drawn over Animal's mind. She awaited her Master's instructions.

Ipsissimus wiped his fat lips on a pure white napkin, starched stiff. He sighed contentedly. He liked that napkin, liked leaving gravy stains from his lips upon it. He was the only one of the company to be laid a place with such a napkin. It separated him from the others, and he liked that.

'Now, Est,' he said with careful deliberation, 'we must go over this house together and make preparations. You don't seem the same person as you were before.' He implied he had not been attracted to her before but now was.

'I'm richer,' she said simply as they rose from the meal. He with full belly, she with empty. She was amazed that she was going along with him, amazed that she was sexually curious. `

Ipsissimus smirked, 'Gold.' He rubbed his hands together and showed her his teeth. She didn't understand why this gesture made her think, 'Prick.' and 'Want his.' Was this an irresponsible inclination?

Polly and Claudia rushed in, 'Mama said something about dessert.'

'Dessert *and* washing up.' It was a relief for Est to play the natural part of mother.

'Do we have to?'

'You don't have to, but if you don't cooperate in the running of the household, then the household may not want to cooperate in the running of your life,' Est nagged comfortably.

'Alright.'

'Great. There are meringue bombs on the sideboard. Mama's specials.'

'All for us?' The girls admired the individual dishes laid out in a row, white with sugar, tangy with raspberries, plump with cream.

'Don't stuff yourselves. Please.'

Ipsissimus moved in on the dessert; he had a sweet tooth. 'I will bring two bowls with us upstairs?' Ipsissimus enticed Est. He held two bowls ceremoniously as he left the room. Est shrugged to Claudia; she would go with him.

'I'll be down at nine to check the kitchen and get you two to bed. Alright?'

'Nine o'clock? That's too early,' whined Claudia.

'Not too early to be in bed. You can read and chat for a while. If you go to bed any later you'll never get enough sleep for school tomorrow. And I don't think Polly's mother would be pleased about that.'

Ipsissimus had gone on ahead, a procession of one.

'You've got more than an hour to play.' Exercising parental responsibility brought her back to earth. She loved her daughter.

Listening to the echo of Ipsissimus's feet, it dawned on her that he was going to the Crystal Room. 'Where Stritch and I..., the room where Stritch and I...'

A fat white ringed hand passed through her mind and swept these thoughts away. Relaxed, Est happily followed the lead of Ipsissimus's feet.

8.2 Meringue

Claudia and Polly washed up as fast as possible, which was not very fast as it involved splashing each other with soap suds. Mama Shag tidied the kitchen and attended to poor Hound No. 5 and poor Animal.

Inert Animal would not have been able to respond even if her fairy godmother had turned up and asked, 'What is your heart's desire, my child?' Her shabby cotton frock could have been transformed to a sumptuous red satin ball gown and Animal would not have noticed. The complex subtleties of her body had been annihilated and replaced with one dominant impulse, Ipsissimus and the Great Work.

The zenith of this impulse was in the developing foetus thickening Animal's waist a touch, to accommodate its growth. She didn't exactly *know* she was pregnant, a mother to be, she simply heard the pulse 'Ipsissimus, Ipsissimus,' louder, clearer than ever and was reassured. She was more certain than ever that she was on the right path, the path of brilliance lit by the stellar glow of her very own star. As *he* always said, 'Every man and woman is a star.' She sat content at the table, inattentive to the small Thelemic world and its events, proceeding around her.

'Animal.' Mama Shag put her strong arm around Animal's shoulders and spoke close to her ear. Mama focussed her magickal mind. 'Animal.'

With a last flourish of the mop, Claudia and Polly emptied the sink. They dashed over to the sideboard and hastily took two bowls of tempting meringue pudding each and rushed off to the Ballroom, only too pleased to get away from kitchen weirdness.

'She gives me the creeps.' Claudia sat on the low window sill. Behind her the shutters had not yet been closed, they squeaked and rattled slightly.

'Me too.' The sweet pudding provided a shield from scary things.

'Imagine having her as your mother!' Polly shuddered, remembering Animal's wild staring eyes.

'Don't even think it. Oops!' Claudia dropped a piece of creamy meringue on her bottle green V-necked school jumper. She scraped it off with a licked spoon, leaving the merest trace of fat. They saw their reflections in the window mixed with the view of lawn, ha-ha and fountain.

'I think the fountain's stopped.' Polly squinted to see better. She spread her fingers upon the window.

'It often gets clogged up. Especially when he's here.' Claudia wrinkled up her nose.

'I thought he was quite nice.' Polly pressed her face against the glass, squashing her nose. 'It's started working again.'

'Quite nice! You don't know what you're talking about!' Claudia exclaimed angrily. She set to work on her second bowlful of pudding.

'I thought he was polite and distinguished. Elegant too, quite a gentleman. It's still going,' she added, straining to hear the irregular lurch of water falling into water.

'You may think that now, but wait till you get to know him.' Claudia continued to pounce upon comforting confectionary.

'I'd like to.' Polly was strangely grown-up with contemplative sophistication.

'You give me the creeps.' Claudia thumped her. 'You'll turn into Animal.' She sat still with a zombie bland face, in imitation of Animal.

'I won't.' Polly thumped her back.

'You will.'

'I won't.'

'Alright you won't. I'm glad you won't. But look out for Beast or God or whatever he wants to call himself.'

'He said to me, "You can call me..." ' Polly's voice adopted the aloof adult tone that unsettled Claudia, who butted in, mimicking.

'You can call me "devil", you can call me "vampire, ghoul, cannibal". I'll give you nightmares and you'll turn into Animal and you'll thank me for it and end up having a baby when you're 14 and your mother will throw you out of home and noone will look after you and you'll end up dying in a ditch soaking wet with a baby crying beside you like some creepy fairy tale.'

Claudia cocked her head to one side then ran off to the piano. She had amazed herself almost as much as she'd amazed Polly with this speech.

'Is there any more of that pudding?' Polly asked.

'Might be.' Claudia thumped a few piano keys, inexpertly.; then softened her touch, to splendidly fill the big room with simple music.

'If you want more pudding,' she said as she played, 'you'll have to go into the kitchen.'

'I don't mind. Do you want any?'

Claudia shrugged, not really wanting Polly to go but not wanting to tell her what to do either. She felt angry and confused; didn't know how to tell Polly what she knew about that man. Didn't want to tell her either; wanted her just to know, to feel it as all wrong without her having to say anything. As Polly collected up the bowls and padded quietly out of the room, the floorboards creaked under her feet. Claudia's hands lay still on the keys.

She wanted to get up and follow Polly but knew Polly didn't want her to. As Polly left the room she tiptoed to peek through the crack between door and door jamb. It was a moment or two before the scene framed by a large wooden settle and a free standing bookcase came into focus. Claudia smelt dark old wood and ancient polish and there was Polly young and alive and walking slowly, quietly, an empty pudding bowl in each hand. Walking not down the corridor to the kitchen, but up the oak stairs to the bedrooms.

'She'll know now,' Claudia whispered to herself. She wanted to go away from this place with Est. Get a long way away from *Ridelands* and a long way from him.

8.3 Too Young

Animal and Mama Shag were the only ones remaining in the quiet kitchen, where a pleasant smell of dinner lingered.

'Turquoise-clad, holding crystal aloft, wood encircling my wrists, silver upon my breast.' Mama Shag calculated a magickal act that would, at least temporarily, pull aside the diaphanous veils that stretched across Animal's mind. She looked into mute Animal's eyes and made the analysis that lilac supernatural mist had accumulated in Animal's mind through excess magickal practice without pause for cleansing and recuperation.

Mama Shag rummaged in a drawer for an aniseed ball. 'Turquoise and silver,' she murmured. She pictured a robe she kept somewhere, with an assigned magickal purpose of summoning spirit into the body. It was not something she would choose to do; to transfer energy from one plane to another while the mind was in a vulnerable state. 'What else can I do? Ipsissimus won't help me,' she chuckled in spite of Animal's lamentable condition. 'I know him too well to expect compassion of any order.'

She indulged in a few backward glances at Animal as she went to find her magickal equipment. She regretted that Animal had refused to come to the garden cavern, 'Where magickal ceremony always goes right.'

Polly heard Mama Shag's heavy foot on the staircase and flattened herself against the corridor wall. She was in shadow as she listened to Mama Shag mutter, 'Turquoise robe, silver, crystal and wood, yes I have it all. Yes, perfume of jasmine.'

As Polly's ears pricked up she also traced other sounds that previously she had not been aware of. The wind outside picked up, creating draughts and rattles around *Ridelands*. She heard little clicking and scratching noises of the house itself and the small creatures living in it, mice, even beetles. There was a sonorous drone, akin to the wash of water behind a canal boat; it was his voice, Ipsissimus's. The voice, she felt, called her specifically, spoke to her inner need.

Mama Shag stopped on the landing and sniffed the air. Polly watched her, her heart beating with the excitement of guilty secretiveness. She pressed her body closer against the wall. Her cheek tingled on the chill plaster; her eyes flickered in agitation as Mama Shag remained on the landing, silent and alert.

'She knows I'm here,' Polly thought. She still held a pudding bowl in each hand; one of them clanged against the wall. Mama Shag pivoted round. 'She's staring straight into my eyes.' As indeed Mama Shag was, but Mama was in magickal mode. Yes, she did look straight and deep into Polly's eyes but she did not think in a mundane way, 'There is Polly hiding in the shadows, what is she doing there?'

Coloured waves flowed through Mama's mind, linked her soul to other such aware souls. She saw, 'Fuchsia, purple, green, guilt unseen, unneeded, a neophyte, the beginning of a quest.' She saw Polly's desire for knowledge and initiation. She did not see her as a 12 year old girl she had a duty to protect. She was not a girl to Mama Shag at all; she was waves of coloured energy participating in the rhythm of Mama Shag's magick.

Mama Shag proceeded to her apartment more composed and confident than before her encounter with Polly's soul, to collect a turquoise shining robe, plus silver, crystal and wood accessories.

Polly's face was very white and she trembled compulsively, consequently dropping both pudding bowls. The spoons clattered out first; the bowls followed but did not break. Mama Shag was out of earshot (whether actually or psychological is open to question).

The drone of Ipsissimus's ritual chant continued, sounding like the working rumble of an efficient engine.

The occasional pause for breath broke up the robotic affect with a degree of organic irregularity.

Polly shook from head to foot, absolutely immobilised, for the time being at least. She listened to the drone, no irregularities now, it was one long unbroken hum. Polly slumped to the floor; her neck flopped to the side, her hands and feet twitched nervously.

Two doors away was Ipsissimus:

'I am Ankh-af-na-Khonsu, priest of the 26th dynasty.
Proven by the zealousness of my path to purity.
Proven by the containment of my human talents
into this my Priestly self.
Essence of truth and wisdom.
Lord of this world beyond time and space,
Alive yet dead, speaking and yet silent.

'I am Ankh-af-na-Khonsu, priest, and I bring to you the wisdom of the Stele of Revealing, the Stele which commemorates my very own death. Yet here I am, alive and virile through the power of the words that were carved upon the Stele.

Thus do I reveal to you the magickal energies at my command through the inscription upon my Stele.'

Ipsissimus raised his arms before the crystal prisms on the altar in the Crystal Room and pointed his index fingers down. Dark shapes buffeted his mind; supernatural light burnt in his eyes.

'Ixaxaar! Sixty stone!' he called; an unspeakable sound replete with inhuman foreboding. 'Ixaxaar,' the sound of fire feeding on an impossible fuel of water. In the corridor, Polly's solitary form twitched in small nervous tics which gathered momentum as Ipsissimus continued.

'My Ixaxaar, my Stele of Revealing, I will reveal now what was revealed by my very own death, I Ipsissimus, I Ankh-af-na-Khonsu!

> 'I am the inspired Lord of Thebes
> I watch as mysteries relinquish their veils,
> For me, Ankh-af-na-Khonsu.
>
> 'I control my own life,
> My words are truth,
> Ra-Hoor-Khuit! I invoke you.
>
> 'You! Lord of Intense Unity!
> I adore your virile breath.
> You inspire terror,
> You make Death tremble,
> I adore you.
>
> 'Appear on the throne of Ra
> Open the ways of Khu,
> Lighten the way of Ka,
> The way of the Khuhs run through me,
> To stir or still me.
> Aum, fill me!
>
> 'Aum, aum, aum.'

Sound without end or beginning, strong and compelling.

Polly's body that had been convulsed dangerously while Ipsissimus spoke as Ankh-af-na-Khonsu, priest of the 26th Egyptian dynasty, now rested easy, though her open eyes darted now one way, now another.

Ipsissimus continued mesmerically:

'Ra-Hoor-Khuit, son at midnight,
Crowned and conquering child
Come and breathe upon me,
Breathe with all your inestimable virility
That I may be an embodiment of your virile virtue.

'You fill me, I feel you, you fill me, I feel you.'

Ipsissimus breathed fast through his nose, making a singular hissing noise. Simultaneously his lingam filled with blood and became hard and yet harder still. As hard as a sex god's? As hard as Ra-Hoor-Khuit's?

This was when Est played her part in the plot. She had prepared herself for this before, at Cefalù. But whether it had been fear of being upstaged, magickal constipation or cowardice, Ipsissimus had always, at the last moment, cried off performing the ritual with Est, ostensibly due to a severe bout of asthma. Each time this had happened Est had secretly been relieved, while Ipsissimus retreated to the treatment of his breathless condition with heroin and cocaine.

He had breath today. The breath of the mighty Ra-Hoor-

Khuit rose strong in the priest Ankh-af-na-Khonsu, received by our beloved, yet somehow pessimistic Ipsissimus. How other than pessimistic if you had to apply to a little known god for an erection?

Est should have now said her bit, from the state of trance she should have been in, to be followed by an act of sexmagick with Ipsissimus, embodying the Priest Ankh-af-na-Khonsu. Manifestation would be completed by the Priest's seminal emission and its subsequent commingling with the magickal secretions (16 kalas) that had been collecting within the Priestess's yoni.

Unfortunately for this Working, nothing had been collecting in Est's cunt. She was not turned on at all. She had been when she'd followed him up here from the kitchen, but this room and the robe and memories of Stritch had brought her down. The room smelt of old cunt, someone else's cunt. She felt like just another priestess and anonymity did not arouse her. Also, Ipsissimus was old and ugly, his cheeks flabby and even though his eyes were luminous, it was a deathly glow, like that of a radioactive isotope.

She was too much the analytical artist to be taken over by his charisma. He seemed kinky to her, a pervy old man who needed occult paraphernalia to get it on. Like some men needed dogs and others arse; this one needed games with gods.

Ipsissimus had not noticed that his chosen priestess was basically just sitting on a crystal step chewing her nails and tugging nervously at a strand of hair. From time to time she wrestled with a piece of dead skin on the side of a finger; she was more in tune with her internal dialogue than to a reincarnated priest of the 26th dynasty of Ancient Egypt.

Ipsissimus had not noticed her lack of magickal attention, because he felt the presence of the priestess and her readiness for his erection. He visualised the secretions of the 16 kalas, fresh and plentiful, the waters of eternal life uninterruptedly flowing.

He turned from the expansive window; his robe was significantly raised at crotch level by his steaming erection.

'She is come,' he pronounced. 'She has flowed into her form, she is come.'

From her position prone on the corridor floor Polly, 12 years old, arose and moved, in trance, towards the door to the Crystal Room. Her hand was upon the handle she shook ecstatically, virginally, as she entered the Crystal Room.

'My Priestess is come.' He did not see the girl in school uniform; he saw the answer to his prayers.

Est looked on nervously. 'What is this?' she asked herself, alarm growing as Polly swayed and Est noted her lack of girlish self-possession.

'No.' Est mouthed, 'No.' Ipsissimus pulled his robe over his head and came to stand before his Priestess absolutely naked with a steamer on, virile as a god. He came close to Polly, the tip of his lingam brushed the waistband of her skirt.

'Remove thy raiment, oh Priestess of the Temple,' he intoned mesmerically.

Est watched, astounded, paralysed, as Polly reached the back of her skirt and began to unfasten her buttons. Fortunately they were stiff and awkward and it was not going to be easy for Polly to disrobe; this gave Est some thinking time.

'No!' she called louder. Neither Priest nor Priestess responded. 'No!' she repeated as she stood up.

The air was very still. Then came sudden heat, as though air itself were sweating. Vapour pulsed out into the hot atmosphere as if a source of noisome gas had just been exposed. It was thick and yellow; it smelt of sulphur and made her cough. She couldn't see Polly, nor could she see that dreadful erection. She groped for the door to open it, to let in air, but the door was already open.

The Priest clasped the Priestess to him, stroked her hair, unaffected by the yellow fog, protected from this veil of putrescence by Ra-Hoor-Khuit, in order that Ipsissimus could honour the god.

Est groped about her; her hands clutched at empty handfuls of smog. Then she felt the forms of the clasped pair. Neither Priest nor Priestess reacted as her hands explored them. She could feel that Polly was still dressed. Est's limbs were weak, hardly obeying her Will. She couldn't move Ipsissimus, couldn't push them apart, couldn't stop him. She could only see one option open to her, to save Polly. She rushed from the room, to find Mama Shag and to bring her in here, to wake Polly up from this nightmare.

In her haste she tripped in the corridor. What was this? Rather who, as she bent down and peered into a white face.

'Polly,' she called gently. The girl was sweating, her cheeks red, her lips parted. 'Polly,' she stroked her straight hair. A draught of hot air gushed out from the Crystal Room and blew down the corridor at speed, the door slammed behind it. It passed over Polly's body and the atmosphere became icy. Est saw an orange light enter Polly. Then the girl stretched in an ordinary waking up kind of way. A voice in Est's mind, not her own, called, 'Ixaxaar, a game I play with God. It was never real.'

Polly, somewhat dumbfounded, blushed as she picked up the two pudding bowls.

'I must have fallen over,' she said hesitantly, not knowing whether she was lying or telling the truth. She was confused at what the truth was, out of her depth in current circumstances.

'Did you want some pudding?' Est asked. 'Come to the kitchen, love. Then I think you and Claudia ought to be getting to bed. Is Claudia still in the Ballroom?' Est continued, soothingly. 'The other way to the kitchen is closed off now. We found the door got left open and created a through draught.'

Polly leant heavily upon Est as they slowly descended the stairs. Claudia joined them in the hall.

'Did you get your pudding then?' Claudia asked, bitchily. Est shot her a *don't ask* look.

8.4 Substitute Whore

Est gently escorted Polly to the kitchen for goodnight cocoa. Ipsissimus's monotone passed through her mind, 'I knew she wasn't real - it was never real - it should have been you - it should be you - no harm done - it will be you.'

Est scowled. 'Why does he always have to be self-centred, trite and secretive?' His secretiveness was as attractive to her as it was potentially deadly. Trouble was 'deadly' rather attracted her too.

She thought about next week when she was due to bring Maltby home. 'Home?' she queried automatically. 'Here?' Mauve and emerald lights danced around her; their chaotic movement teased and mocked her. They were a sign that Ipsissimus's power was accumulating, his Will focussing in preparation for a Great Work. A magickal conclusion to all he had achieved at Cefalù.

Est would have to think and work fast, to protect Polly

from the twisted opportunities Ipsissimus offered. Why! She'd be selling her soul for loose change and smoking opium rather than attending to her studies. Polly's parents, being mainly absent, working abroad, would hardly notice.

In profound concentration Mama Shag, turquoise-clad, sang sweetly to lull Animal to relaxation, thereby making her open to suggestion. For Mama was aware that where Animal went, Hound No. 5 would follow.

Animal's neck relaxed and her head lolled to one side; relaxation stole over her. The kitchen was bright and warm and smelt wonderfully of cooking, of a whole lifetime of delicious cinnamon cakes and fruit pies. The smell of fresh bread was impregnated into the wood.

'Animal,' Est said sharply, helping Polly into a chair, 'go to Ipsissimus, in the Crystal Room. He's calling you. He says he needs you now. Can't you hear him?'

As if a towering tidal wave loomed up foaming white and mad to crash and break apart dependable walls of the world as we know it; thus came Ipsisimus's voice.

'Babalon, my Scarlet Woman, superb whore of stars,

Your hand is a cup filled with saint's blood.'

Animal stirred and her eyes sparkled. Then a lovely smile lit up her face. She rose to her feet. Hound No. 5 squealed as she drooled on one of his fingers. He made no delay in following her on all fours as Animal's light feet pattered along the corridor, fatefully drawn to the source of the voice, to Ipsissimus.

'From Priestly heart unadulterated desire pours -
And you are ecstatic.

'Faithful virgins die voluntarily for you,
Compulsively, they nourish you,
Whore! More necessary than virtue.

'Worth all goodness in the world,
You are the Great White plane wherein is concealed
The intensity of your scarlet self.

'Here does the graal vessel dwell, door of all doors,
Mystery of all mysteries,
Essence of all essences.'

Joyously Animal joined Ipsissimus in the Crystal Room.
Ipsissimus's arms were outstretched as he faced the bay
window. The room was lit with bright white light; spotlights
were reflected in the floor to ceiling length windowpanes.

No loving look, tender gesture, nor reassuring word
passed between them. They did not consider each another
as ordinary people do. One mystical entity took its place
opposite its complementary mystical entity. At this level
their relationship worked as easily as an idle summer day's
dreaming. Sex was fantastic, their respective orgasms
matchless. Though there was no acknowledgement of this,
no pillow talk no, 'It was great, how was it for you?' No
snuggling down to find the most comfy sleeping position
and no bed.

Today, there was a hard crystal floor, leading to an altar

before the windows, an altar with steps at each side of the room which made its centre something of a pit, a pit, or depressed arena where acts of sexmagick occurred.

'You are come,' Ipsissimus addressed Animal.

Animal pulled her thin frock open in one purposeful gesture and most of the buttons down the front popped off. The dress slid off her white body, she was naked beneath, her form described by veins painfully visible all over her body, even over the extent of her hollow stomach, so thin was she. She had been thin before she fasted and she had been fasting for 12 days. With nil by mouth the Priestess had been prepared. Her chest was child flat, in contrast to her mound of Venus, which was prominent and bony, thickly hairy, a beard of hair hanging in the empty space between her thighs.

'I am come,' Animal answered him. Her voice was croaky and unsure from lack of use. Faithful Hound No. 5, on all fours again, licked her ankles and her feet; he licked her dangling hands and her prominent hip bones. He marked out the contours of her body with a slug slime trail of saliva, while Animal Scarlet Woman and Ipsissimus sexmagickally engaged.

∴nine

9.1 In the Mauvezone

Maltby was seated in a wheel chair, with a blanket over his knees. He was spry and combed and although his sunken cheeks were yellowish, his eyes were alert and intelligent.

From where they sat with the sanatorium behind them, Est looked across the lake below to the definition of mountains beyond. The air was crisp and clear. She felt like a character in someone else's book, or better still, an archetype portrayed in a painting. She squinted in the hard sun, saying in her silence what she didn't want to say out loud.

Maltby examined Est's profile. His heart surged; he adored the strength and compassion he saw there. She was beautiful to him.

'Come back with me.' Est spoke with calm practicality, but visualised pushing Maltby and his wheel chair down the rocky slope, to the lake, the chair gathering momentum. This fantasy was an example of the emotional vertigo she suffered from when faced with responsibility.

She said, 'We can't go back to Paris; I need England. Ipsissimus will carry on with his Thelemic work for a while at *Ridelands*, probably until Mama needs the place for Shrinker Yearly Meeting. Though Ipsissimus will, no doubt, consult his holy guardian angel, Aiwaz, for magickal instructions.' Est stretched while Maltby chuckled in a sane wry way, although laughter ran into coughing. Est rubbed his neck and shoulders.

'Breathe easy and deep through your nose,' she advised soothingly, although her concern for his health bored her.

'I need to paint a canvas as big and simple as this scenery.' She changed the subject. 'Have you noticed how the lake turns everything around it mauve, especially the sky? The mountains are mauve too.'

The lake pulled deeply upon the unconscious, creating an awareness of the abyss in everything perceived.

The mountains' silhouette was clearly defined by a black

outline where it joined the pastel hue of sky. In sunlight mountains' shadow covered half the lake and mauve was lost while stone blocked sun. To see the rainbow coloured subtleties in the reflection of mountain in lake is a lifetime's effort of observation.

Est pointed to the mountain, using the gesture to stretch her spine. There was a practical purpose in everything she did, just as there was esoteric probing in every vision she contemplated.

'I would like you to leave this place.'

'Yes,' agreed Maltby.

'I think you should.'

'Yes.' His eyes followed the flight path of a buzzard.

Est rested her hands either side of his head. She liked it that he was weaker than she, that he had crumbled under Ipsissimus's influence while she had not.

'I shall take you somewhere very beautiful. I shall paint and you shall tell me what you think of my paintings, until it is time for you to sell them.'

'For a fortune.' The buzzard hovered.

Est laughed joyously. 'Yes! A large fortune.'

They looked into each other's eyes. The small fortune to grow into a large fortune. A celebration. A beautiful studio, perhaps on a windy hill, maybe in a sheltered combe, with a stream. Claudia's school somewhere nearby.

Est visualised a studio, with views all around, views of anything, views of the world and views of her dream journeys marked upon canvas. Her ego was a paintbrush as blue coils of creative energy twisted out of her head. Red lines of heat came up from hell into her feet and warmed her ego.

'Come on, let's go inside.' The sun winked as a cloud passed. 'We shall consult these learned doctors of yours,' Est drawled lazily pushing Maltby hard uphill, giving him an exciting, bumpy ride over uneven ground.

The clinic appeared on the lower slope of the mountain. It had been built with a low profile among groups of tastefully placed trees.

'I-can't-get-out-of-this meeting?' stuttered out Maltby.

'I could talk to the doctor alone. Though I think if you're not ready to discuss your illness and your progress, you're not ready to leave.'

'Um.' He sounded doubtful.

'Your throat for instance, is that going to get better? What's wrong with it?'

'Recurring infection,' offered Maltby with evident satisfaction.

'Why won't it clear up? Is it anything serious?'

The entrance door to the clinic was held open for them by a polite, refined figure. She wore a pristine white coat with two pens peeping from the left breast pocket and a nametag with her professional position underneath in small letters, *Staff Manager*. Her self-containment leaked certainty as most of us leak anxiety.

'Doctor Hatzig will be with you in ten minutes. Would you like to wait for him in his office.' The staff manger handed Est a thick file. 'He thought you might like to look at some of this paperwork first.'

'Thank you.' Est handed the file to Maltby as she needed both hands to push the wheel chair. It seemed very modern to be given the file entitled *Health Management* to peruse.

9.2 Sincerity

Est critically regarded a huge turquoise canvas. Tiny figures in silver filigree writhed and cavorted in Celtic intertwining patterns upon a shimmering vessel. Her heart was at peace. The people about her were in relative strategic positions she found convenient and exciting. She had fought for this and would continue to fight; for the continuum of never-ending conflict is the hub of successful alchemy.

She hadn't been able to resist coming here and taking up her paint brushes for the day or two while Maltby got himself settled in The Cottage, actually only a couple of miles away from *Ridelands*. Claudia and Polly would keep an eye on him and visa versa.

Est wore off-white painting trousers, and wiped her silver laden brush on them from time to time, smearing silver trails on the cotton drill. She bit the inside of her lower lip. Somewhere up above, in another part of *Ridelands*, someone was making a lot of noise.

'Those two, Animal and Mahoney, arguing or lovemaking or hashing up one of Ipsissimus's shoddy rituals, half-baked art, half-baked religion. Why am I drawn to him?' She said aloud, 'Don't know.' She tucked loose fronds of growing hair behind her ears. 'Don't know. Something about the way he walks. Something about the way he talks. Something about the way he turns on. Claudia would be disgusted. She'll probably grow up and only like clean living business men with law degrees from Oxford, owning at least five bespoke suits.'

Shrieks of woefully intense lovemaking came from above. It could only be Animal doing her duty for *He* had told her to be with Hound No.5, to initiate him into the next grade of the Thelemic Order.

Part of Ipsissimus's motive in assigning Animal this duty was (as usual) to get the mad girl off his back. The pregnant mad girl, big with child and crazier than ever. She was fleshless, haunted and close to derelict, with bump attached.

Est's attention had wandered a little too far. She stepped back a few paces from the canvas. It always seemed to be evening in this room, she thought. She stepped back again to see how light caught the silver vessel and brought movement to the filigree figures in tiny subtleties of extraterrestrial grace.

While she was thus absorbed, a cold shiver shot kundalini from the base of her spine over the top of her head and into her tongue. She sensed someone behind her, someone she had called to her. She sensed that she could have a piece of the pleasure that made Animal howl.

'Yes, a good vibration.' *He* put his hands on her shoulders, caressed her with the magickal energy he stored within his body. *He* gave her a taste of what he wanted to transmit to her, magickally, ritually, erotically, as only Ipsissimus could.

'Don't you ever think about your responsibilities?' she asked him playfully. Cold rain poured vertically on the grey side of the deep bay window.

His hands rested heavy upon her shoulders. 'Should I laugh?' Est asked him. He was caught in a moment of self-doubt inappropriate to his top magickal grade. Death in life, life in death, the unity of opposites beyond time and space had been the first stage of his journey. He grunted and took an elaborately decorated gold snuff box from a pocket concealed in his white linen undergarment.

He fumbled with the gorgeous gold lid, unsure whether to meet Est's eye or not, as she turned from the graal painting to face him.

'It is not from fear of drunkenness that I am sober,' Est said, eye contact irrelevant for her voice penetrated where no sense organ could reach. She continued:

'It is not from fear of the dark that I stand in the light.

Nor from hatred of the rain - real, actual, present,

That I take sanctuary in this dry studio,

It was not dissatisfaction that drove me to this house.'

Her eyes were narrow. A thin shining slit of eye was revealed communicating the attitude of Aphrodite upon realising that a worker in metals, Hephaestus, was her husband and that he was at work upon a metal net with which to entrap her. How had she become attached to such a man? This Hephaestus, this Ipsissimus?

'Come,' he said, 'the Crystal Room is the right place for us.'

He had chosen his moment well. She was mesmerised by his intention for her; it coincided exactly with her own magickal ambition. Without hesitation or reluctance they made their way to the room of light.

With his back to the altar, he was calm and tranquil. In a gesture of surprising grace, he took a pinch of greyish powder. His bearing was quite different from his previous ham-handedness when he'd grovelled at Est's neat feet for the valuable lid, bearing hieroglyphics from the Stele of Revealing, translating as: 'The self-slain Ankh-af-na-Khonsu - whose words are truth, I invoke thy presence, O Ra-Hoor-Khuit!'

Ra-Hoor-Khuit together with Hoor-Par-Kraat were each one half of a twinned deity, the sun at midnight, Horus - crowned and conquering child.

'Hidden God!' Ipsissimus intoned with great pleasure, such as one experiences after a large pinch of heroin at the right ritual moment of preamble.

The sun sank but the rain beat on. No artificial light had

yet been lit in this hour when all were separately engaged in operations in preparation for the great midnight togetherness. This would mark the start of Ipsissimus's Great Magickal Retirement, when he would be alone to write, perchance to die - in part at least, to slither out of his English gentleman's skin and discover a wilder nature beneath.

The silence of heroin pervaded Ipsissimus. He placed amulets carved from cornelian upon his eyes. 'The voice of silence is found in the stillness of the eyes' pool of contemplation.' Ipsissimus was impressive.

'What has been begotten grew on what would have died, decayed, but for the power of Anubis, god of embalming. Through his power, what was dead has not decayed and what was alive has not grown, but remained as a child, in silent stasis.

'Hidden god, blind as the dead,
your voice is silence.
Hoor-Paar-Kraat,
I honour your absence,
for you are all that is not
and never can be; you are
stasis, absence, silence.

'I celebrate you, for only your
stamina and rock-like stillness
can lead me to Ra-Hoor-Khuit,
who is joyousness and ecstasy overflowing.

Gold and abundance be mine!
So that I may honour you,
Ra-Hoor-Khuit.'

Ipsissimus took up the silk turquoise robe and drew it over his head. He took up the golden headdress and proudly placed it upon his head.

Est: 'I am neither virgin nor spouse,
nor widow nor wench.

'I am woman girt with sword,
I am she who holds the wordless aeon
between her thighs.
My talisman is Ixaxaar, the sixtystone,
an intense, condensed elixir
we shall create.'

Ipsissimus: 'We shall create the talisman,
and you shall come into your power.'

Est: 'Yes!
I am she who passes the sword
between her thighs,
and hides it within her womb.
I am she who knows her own mind.
Bearer of the graal and sword,
I am she.'

Ipsissimus: 'Are you she who bears the hidden god

within her womb?
Are you she who gives life to
the sun at midnight?

'Are you Isis, devoted wife to Osiris?
Mother, beyond reproach
to your twin children -

'Horus Ra-Hoor-Khuit and
Horus Hoor-par-Kraat?

'Are you she through whom
the quartering of the circle
is realised?

'Are you my Scarlet Woman?'

Est: 'Yes!'

Ipsissimus: 'I am he who orders your existence,
I am he who calls you into being.
I am he who recognises your power,
as no other can.
I! He through whom you learn your name.

'Do you acknowledge me?
Do you acknowledge my grade and name
as one - Ipsissimus?
Beyond godhead and divinity
into the new aeon,
into unspeakable dimensions,

always glorious?'

Est: 'Yes!
I have come through
the wrought iron gates of fate;
they have clanged behind me,
I still hear the whine of their unoiled hinges
within my ears.
The aromas of that fate-filled land
behind me, cling to me.
This, my entrance to earth,
is not the beginning of my existence,
for the feeling of Fate is strong within me.
I can smell its autumnal aromas.
I come from another land
and I am bound for another land.

'The carved yew doors are before me,
they mark the entrance to my native land and
tell of the obstacles I must overcome.

'Fate tells me I can pass through these doors.
My mind pauses upon the carvings thereon,
which hold my attention
like a hypnotist's pendulum.

'This place is rich with the light of souls.
The Earth is rich with food;
see how the glossy ants crawl across my toes!'

Ipsissimus: 'Yes! Where the body of the goddess
seeps sugar, there are ants.
When your tears are sweet
with unrequited love,
the translucent amber ants are attracted.
They love the sweet flow of Eros.

'My beloved, you have given me,
wanderer of the wastes,
a home land.
I have fought to describe my self as I am,
white bodied and golden headed.
And when I wear a shroud,
my shroud is turquoise,
and when I wear a mask,
my mask is gold and black.
And when my hands touch life,
that I may rise from my
many layered sarcophagus,
my hands touch stone.
Sapphire stone. Ixaxaar!

'My beloved goddess.
You who secreted sugar and
were pursued by ravenous ants.
You now tread upon the rotten corpses
of truth seekers.
Pinpoints of mauve light irradiate your path.'

Est: 'And have you died and are you now alive?'

Ipsissimus: 'Yes, I know of other lives, other worlds.'

Est: 'As I am dead,
I feel no pleasure
for I have experienced too much pleasure.
I am numb from excess stimulation
for I am whore of whores.
My senses have died in orgasm.
My nerves flow unchecked by need,
in an unadulterated stream.
From beneath the strata of rocks,
energy from the core stone of Earth
flows through me,
unchecked by curiosity.'

Ipsissimus: 'And does the energy return?'

Est: 'Always, the energy comes from Heaven
and descends through my body
and so into Earth.

'I am the vessel for solar-phallic power
and my nerves are excited.
I am woman carrying the solar-phallic rays.
I am hot and red with the heat of the sun.
I am Scarlet Woman.'

Ipsissimus: 'And what of Earth? What of her power?
Can you feel Hecate alive within you?'

Est: 'The chthonic flow of water is tidal
            and irresistible.
            Water flows around the stone
            and pulls all to her.
            To drown is to die and die within Earth I will.
            I am supple, pulled this way and that
            by the pull and eddy of dynamic water.'

Ipsissimus: 'Ixaxaar.'

Est: 'Ixaxaar.'

Ipsissimus: 'What are you, noble whore?'

Est: 'I am a vessel filled with blood,
            from which only blood can flow.
            I am chaos, I am guilt,
            I am jealousy and ravenous hunger.
            I am a host of suicides clamouring for blood.
            I am the blood lust of the multitude,
            I am the hunger for war.
            I am Scarlet Woman.'

Ipsissimus: 'And you are mine.'

Est: 'If you are my Ipsissimus
            then I am your Scarlet Woman.
            Are you my Ipsissimus?'

Ipsissimus: 'What is Ipsissimus?'

Est: 'Everything you do is easy, too easy.
   For you cannot live in the present
   as mortal man should.
   'You are immortal but not because
   you are pure and good.
   Nor because you are evil and bad.'

Est poured herself a glass of 1929 Burgundy from the silver jug upon the altar. Her cheeks were red and flushed with excitement. Her hands gesticulated to emphasise the meaning of the chthonic stream of words which flowed from her mouth.

Est: 'You are aloof from good.'

She took a previously prepared heroin laden hypodermic syringe. She rolled back the capacious sleeve of Ipsissimus's shimmering turquoise robe and expertly raised a vein. She tightened the robe to act as tourniquet around his bicep.

A vein stood to attention, purple with his heart's pulse. Est pierced his vein with the fine needle and unleashed the powerful opiate. With the invasion of heroin into his body, Ipsissimus relaxed into the death-in-life freedom which heroin offers the truth seeker and magician-artificer.

Est: 'Neither right nor wrong,
   good nor evil satisfied you,
   you wanted both and yet neither.
   And that - both and neither -
   you wanted simultaneously.

And you found what you searched for
and became this unique being,
Ipsissimus, blind to the present,
blind to mundanity.
Dangerously blind, stupidly insensitive.
You cannot sense whether it is air,
fire or water you move within,
for you do not understand the movements
your body makes.
You are utterly unaware
that you abide within a body,
yet you know you do
You are Ipsissimus. Dead to the present,
you can hardly breathe.
You have outgrown your own fateful purpose
You are death in life, Ipsissimus.'

Ipsissimus: 'I need you, that is all I know.'

9.3 Mauve Destiny

In the West Wing Animal clung to Hound No. 5 and her eyes shone. Then her eyelids closed and she arched her back, thrusting her mount of Venus further up to let him deeper in her vulva. She opened her thighs wider, felt his lingam plunge rhythmically along the ecstatic multitude of internal nerve endings.

Meanwhile in the Crystal Room Est and Ipsissimus continued their Working.

Ipsissimus: 'In spilling my semen I will be Ra-Hoor-Khuit. Luscious Est, I shall spill semen. Would you like me to shag you?'

Est, in a long golden robe shot through with flickering green thread, was majestic before the grand bay window of the Crystal Room. Ipsissimus, behind her, held her shoulders and brought his godlike erection close against the curvaceous swell of her voluptuous buttocks.

'It is time,' he whispered into her ear. He kissed her neck

passionately. He carefully removed a few strands of her hair from his mouth.

'Fairest mystery of them all, come to the altar and drink. We shall do justice to divine purpose.' He stepped away from her to give her time and space. He waited in the total concentration and sublime relaxation of heroin.

She had the idea to turn around, be a petty human and say, 'How can you stand there in that stupid robe and kiss my ear? This is supposed to be magick; this is supposed to be different. But it's the same. The same as I've always been. I looked for you for so long and here you are and here I am. But you're no better and no worse than Stritch, no, nor Pet. Yet it is you here with me, not them. You and I, not Vomit or Animal. Why are people dead? Why are folk mad? Did they have to be, for us to be here?'

A lump of emotion rose in her throat and broke up the barrier of inhibition she had believed would never go away. She felt inhibition disintegrate as fierce passion infused her being, stronger than life itself, a passion that broke up belief and broke up the hold belief had upon her.

When she'd first met Drummond, the Beast, after much . yearning for him, he'd been such a disappointment. She had wanted him to be like Stritch, young, beautiful, anorexic, full of chaotic emotions and naïve virility. Stritch had worshipped her.

The past was dead and gone, this magickal working with Ipsissimus was her destiny. They were side by side before the altar. Two large goblets full of Burgundy stood upon the altar. One was ancient bronze girt with jade and topaz, the other ebony inlaid with ivory.

'Which shall you choose?'

'I choose not to choose,' answered Est. 'I shall manifest and all will be spontaneous. I shall come into my power and you shall shag me any which way.'

Ipsissimus laughed, happy to the roots of his belief system, satisfied with every symbol he had ever investigated and introduced to his fateful reference system.

She took the ebony and ivory cup and flung it and its Greek scenes into the arena before the altar; it skidded on the shiny surface. Here had been enacted ritual dramas witnessed by many extraterrestrial entities, often to the tune of the howls of the Hounds of Hell.

'It begins.' Est took the bronze goblet as Hound No. 5's distant ecstasy was expressed in bestial howls echoing throughout *Ridelands*. Animal entered her own land of orgasm. Hound No. 5 pumped harder, he could not feel any negative side to this unholy lovemaking. It was purely blissful; it was what he had always wanted. It involved his conscious desires and the regenerating thrust of his unconscious. He was living out his Fate while creating a memory he had always dreamt as a beyond life impossibility. Gleefully, he howled. The physical action of shagging was effortless; bliss carried him on. Hound No. 5 howled, Animal howled.

Est held the second cup to Ipsissimus's lips. The

Burgundy from the first-flung cup spread across the crystal arena. As it evaporated a figure emerged in complex twists, as if a human being were struggling through a difficult passageway.

Ipsissimus drained the cup. 'Come to us, brother. You are welcome, you are needed.' And before their very eyes stood Stritch in black shirt and torn white trousers. This figure, that had formed from the vapour of spilt wine, shuddered, before stepping out of the crimson mist, fully formed. Blood seeped through the many cuts in his trousers. He looked around as if surprised to find himself here. He examined his fingers and wriggled them to check they moved. He touched himself and dabbed a finger into wet blood. He sniffed the blood and then shied away from it. Finally he licked the blood.

He looked younger than before, slightly imbecile.

A bright ring of red light whizzed around the room at eye level. Stritch stood on one leg, grinning inanely as a pool of blood collected around his feet.

A wave of nausea choked Est. Ipsissimus was ecstatic; his eyes were lit with immortal intensity. He raised an arm in a big joyful gesture of welcome. 'Let the feast begin. Come, my Immortal Consort.' He took her hand, medieval dance fashion. He held her gently by the fingers; awareness of her beauty liberated him. His body was awash with abandon. His soul was perfect; his Will fully engaged in freeflow of the unconscious.

Elsewhere there was a war in the world. Here, the great

feast of tomorrow would be created in memories of this day. The reverberation of this day's memory would bring fresh chaos and carry future society beyond a moral survivalist behavioural framework, towards the free fall of radical isolation.

'Let us eat. Let us feast.'

'I am your Immortal Consort.' Est's voice was hollow as if reverberating around an empty auditorium, like a tape recording of Queen Elizabeth II as a young girl reciting clear rehearsed words to a nation at war. The pure ringing notes of one absolutely protected from an unnameable contamination: the contamination of the Beast; for always and eternally the Beast will out and illuminate our souls with knowledge from the stars.

'Are you Ipsissimus, as I am Scarlet Woman, she who rules? Otherwise I am his lover.' She inclined her head regally to Stritch.

'I am he. All is as it should be. Let us eat.' With exaggerated formality, Ipsissimus indicated that they should descend to the Crystal Arena where white faced Stritch awaited.

Ipsissimus and Est took their places either side of Stritch, like a pair of overprotective parents beside their dying anorexic child.

'Sex, Love, Magick! I am ravished, and it is Magick that has ravished me.' Ipsissimus touched the blood that seeped from a small incision in Stritch's left thigh. He licked the blood from his fingers. 'Try it. It is good. Blood flows from the sacred sword wound. Fill your cup with blood, that we may drink.'

'I can't drink his blood,' Est protested gently enough to imply willingness and assent.

'Why not?' His tone assumed that she would drink. He simply wished to indulge her slight aversion, all the more to revel in her final acquiescence.

'He would die.' A small objection.

'He is dead already.' Of course! How easy life became when one was dead! Anything was possible for no consequences would proceed; the worst had already happened. All actions existed pure in themselves, alone, unnumbered, for here in the Crystal Chamber there was no life. The ritual demanded that this be so, in order that the ritual participants be free as unmade stars.

An intricate atmosphere of occult conspiracy had been nurtured into being. The Thelemites were fellow members of not just any old occult sect; they had access to the blue print for the future aeon.

Est held her brass cup to the open wound on Stritch's left thigh. She pressed its cold metal against his grass and earth stained jeans. The cup filled quickly with living blood from her dead lover.

Ipsissimus and Est drank from the cup, taking quick sips and passing it eagerly from one to the other. Their heads were bent together and their bodies shielded the cup. The blood frothed and foamed as they drank, until, with the last sips, their throats burnt. They screamed and held their hands to throats. In pain they ran around the crystal arena like headless chickens.

'Eat my flesh,' offered Stritch calmly. 'Gnaw upon my bones. The stuff of my body is the only antidote to the stuff of my blood.'

The two headless chickens gawped at him. He was now the rational competent one. The child had defeated his parents.

'Eat me; I taste good.' They gawped. His voice came harder, 'Eat me!'

Authoritative, a command again: 'Eat me.' Seeing them move towards him, registering that they would comply, he softened his voice, and apologised, 'I know there is not much tender meat left upon me. However, my lingam remains.'

Est struggled with his stiff fly button. She began to cry as she did so, remembering the times they'd made love while he was still alive, remembering the emotions of it, the transcendent intensity of it, the transformative power of his body. Crying because she couldn't humanly have him; could have this, these movements towards utter orgasm.

She pulled his trousers down over his emaciated frame. His cock was erect, providing the only impediment to the progress of his trousers down his body. It was huge in comparison to the rest of him, bigger than his arms, fatter and stronger than his thighs. More blood contained there than the rest of his body put together. Stritch's need for satisfaction was strong. He was insistent that his needs be met, in the manner he conceived them. He communicated this message through his massive lingam.

Est knelt. Stritch's lingam brushed her tear-stained face. His lingam's skin was fine and silky; its whole length was strung along with nerve cells and reacted to the barest touch of her skin, of her tears. She craved more reaction. She nuzzled Stritch's lingam with her nose, her lips. Salt tears mingled with musky scented fluid that leaked, drop by frugal drop, from its tip. She loved the red head of his rod, adored its mushroom shape which inspired her to hallucinations and imaginative journeys into the meaning of life and death, inspired her along the path to utter orgasm.

'Stritch, make love to me.' She wanted the passion of his eyes, but encountered blackness with a lingam rising up out of it and into her face, filling her throat.

'He can't,' Ipsissimus declared. 'But I can.' Ipsissimus cupped Est's face tenderly in his paws. 'It is my endless love that manifested him. He is a part in my great drama and how well he plays his part. Look upon him. He is skeletal yet you drool because there is something about him that reminds you of all the dreams you have ever dreamt and that something about him is me.

'It is too late to recapitulate,' Ipsissimus continued, noticing that Est crept away from Stritch, dragging her kneeling form through the pool of blood.

'You cannot turn away from me. All you need and want

to be, is linked to who I am. Hush.' Ipsissimus put a finger to his lips as she opened her mouth to argue. Her curious eyes met his full on, unflinching. Yes, she was brave, braver than he.

'Listen,' Ipsissimus continued, 'listen to the music of the spheres and to your inner needs. Listen to the two and find the similarities. I can unite your inner music with the harmony of the cosmos. Harmony! Cacophony! It is all the same to the gods so long as the orgasm is superb.

'Whore brimming with beauty, elegance, art, come to me and we will make magick.

'Come, let me smell behind your ears. Let me inhale the subtle geranium of your leonine locks. My breath will speak of life to you. I will pour an invisible stream of electricity into you. Invisible! It can only be felt, felt with your sex. Feel my tongue as it discovers your body. Feel my lingam, my Priest's penis, press godlike against you. You will be full of Ipsissimus's orange splendour.

'I must live forever and you must help me. Feel my lingam against your strong thigh.' He eased some of her hair out from where it was caught in her clothing. Each small tug on a strand felt to Est like a current of electricity. In each moment of energy she regretted her whole life and wanted to live it over again. Until this sensation was so oft repeated she became the nature of regret itself and lived her life over and over at speed. Everything about her life, each tiny emotion was clearly defined as Ipsissimus stroked her hair. The strands fell through his fingers.

'Yes,' she said. 'Yes.' Her eyes wide, the veins in her throat erect and hard.

'Disrobe, Priestess, Whore, Scarlet Woman, disrobe.' Ipsissimus entreated.

'Yes.' She pulled her clothes off this way and that, not noticing what the garments were, which meant disrobing took longer. She struggled with clothes entangled around sweating limbs. Finally she was naked. She murmured her ritual words and sweated hot sex sweat. Her sex stench filled the room as her murmurs rose in crescendo:

> 'Disrobing, I'm disrobing,
> I can't sleep, I can't count sheep.
> I can't sleep and I can't count sheep.
> Disrobing, I'm disrobing.'

Ipsissimus followed the contours of her body with his hands. She stood on a crystal stair above him and their groins were level. Their union would take place standing up. Instinctively animal, the lingam nosed its way inbetween her furry lips. Est swung her hips up so the head could make its way into her. With a fast gasp her inner self burst into flame. Each coital rock was a fuel to her fire.

> 'Disrobing, I'm disrobing.'

It was as if all the points of view she had ever had, all attitudes and opinions fell away from her, like discarded snakeskin. She intoned:

'I wore a white coat and black nurse's belt.
I wore a tailored black plastic dress.
I wore a grey pinafore tunic.
And then I wore my lingerie.

Disrobing, I'm disrobing.

Oyster silk bikinis,
mermaid's pallor, it was green,
it had frills.'

And in the background of their sexmagickal standing up shag, came a high pitched desperate scream, the scream of a young rabbit struck in the jugular by a weasel. It was Stritch. Blood bubbled in the back of his throat. Something had changed: since he died he had not felt pain, but now he did; excruciating, intensifying as more and more bits of Est, all the reference points of her being, participated in this erotic rite.

Stritch screamed. Bitter, despairing pain ripped through him and he ran from the room feeling as if his limbs were melting and dripping from him one by one, bit by bit.

'It had frills,' continued Est, as if she heard nothing.
'It felt like the sea,
but it was skin, until the rough lace
felt like a change of air,
felt like the secrets girls can share.

Suck harder.'

Ipsissimus's mouth moved to her nipples.

'Suck harder, suck.

Suck harder.'

-:- **FINIS** -:-

occult high

Printed in the United Kingdom
by Lightning Source UK Ltd.
100555UKS00001B/4-21